Twelfth Night
at
Longbourn

Maria Grace

White Soup Press

Published by: White Soup Press

ISBN-10: 0615938981
ISBN-13: 978-0615938981 (White Soup Press)

Author's Website: RandomBitsofFaascination.com
Email address: Author.MariaGrace@gmail.com

Dedication

For my husband and sons.
You have always believed in me.

" I have been a selfish being all my life, in practice, though not in principle. As a child I was taught what was right, but I was not taught to correct my temper. I was given good principles, but left to follow them in pride and conceit...I was spoilt by my parents, who, though good themselves...allowed, encouraged, almost taught me to be selfish and overbearing; to care for none beyond my own family circle; to think meanly of all the rest of the world; to wish at least to think meanly of their sense and worth compared with my own. Such I was...and such I might still..."

- Jane Austen, *Pride & Prejudice*

Stop by and visit the *Twelfth Night at Longbourn* Pinterest board to see some of the dresses and Regency era items that inspired the book.

http://www.pinterest.com/mariagrace423/twelfth-night-at-longbourn/

Chapter 1

What is right to be done cannot be done too soon, particularly when wrong has already been done.

December 15, 1811

ELIZABETH ROSE AND GLIDED to her husband's side. The soft rustle of her skirts and the scratch of his pen filled the otherwise quiet room. She stood behind him and waited. He would look up soon enough. If she disturbed him, he would spoil the wet ink and insist on beginning again. Unlike Mr. Bingley, he could not abide sloppy letters.

Darcy signed with a flourish and set his pen aside. A quick dusting of sand and he turned to her.

"Oh, my dear." She cradled his face between her palms.

He pulled her into his lap and wrapped his arms around her, lips curving up in the dimpled smile she coveted. "Did I ever tell you how brilliant you were to suggest we share an office?"

"Perhaps, once or twice." His dimples still set her heart aflutter. Hopefully, they always would.

He kissed her, lingering in the sweetness of their embrace. Was it wrong to be disappointed when he stopped and leaned his cheek on top of her head?

"You work too hard."

"You tell me often enough. Before you ask, yes, I am interviewing secretaries. One or two of the candidates may prove worthy. But," he tapped the tip of her nose with his finger, "the work I am doing now is not something even the best secretary could assist with."

"Mrs. Reynolds brought another large stack of letters. A number appear to be social correspondence. May I help—"

"Yes." He pressed her into his chest, scooped up a stack of letters, lumpy with wax seals, and dropped them in her lap.

"That took considerable deliberation." She snickered and picked up the topmost missives. "Are you sure all of these are for me?"

"No, but it matters little. I can think of no business I would keep from your sight."

She pulled back and met his gaze, eyebrow lifted. "So there is no correspondence you might wish to hide—"

Darcy threw his head back and laughed.

How she loved that sound, rich with warmth and tenderness. Perhaps in the next year she might present him with a child, a son he could teach to laugh the same way. Babyish giggles echoing his laughter tickled the back of her mind. The corners of her lips crept upwards.

He kissed her hair. "Dear woman, I already arranged your Christmastide gifts. I have not forgotten."

She tapped his chest. "You are very smug, Mr. Darcy. If you only knew how Papa—"

"I am certain your father owes you a great deal. I hope his marital harmony does not suffer because Kitty alone remains at Longbourn to remind him of what he might have overlooked."

"Oh, poor Kitty! Her letters have been so melancholy since Lydia—"

Darcy gripped her hands. "My dearest, I wish I could have been there as I was for Georgiana."

"Even you cannot protect us all." She touched her forehead to his. "It is done and there is no remedy. We all thought she had learned from…her previous experiences. Even Mr. Bradley and Mr. Pierce agreed that she would be unlikely to repeat her ill-advised attempts to get a husband. I suppose the weight of three sisters married overcame her better judgment. At least Lt. Harper is a gentleman's son."

"He is a second son, and his father has almost nothing to give him."

"I know." She pressed her face into his shoulder. "Still, it is not your responsibility. Papa must bear his share of accountability for the ghastly affair."

"Even so, Kitty should not." Darcy blew out a ragged breath. "Meryton society has judged her harshly despite her having no role in Lydia's elopement."

Elizabeth studied him. The dear man was considering something, weighing out all its possibilities and permutations. He would not be hurried through these deliberations, so she cuddled close. If nothing else, this was a pleasant way to learn patience.

"Georgiana and her new companion will journey to Pemberley for Twelfth Night. I expect this time alone in London has improved her and she will be ready for more diverse company. What say you we invite Kitty to visit as well? Derbyshire is unaware of Lydia and her indiscretions. I expect Kitty might be able to make some new friends and enjoy the society Lambton and Pemberley can offer."

"You are also concerned Georgiana might be lonely when she returns?"

"I am. Miss Lackley has a suitor now, leaving little time for Georgiana. Let us not forget, *you* have impressed upon me the value of sisterly companionship."

"Are you prepared to manage the energy of two young ladies amidst all the entertaining we must do this season?" She stroked his cheek.

"They might be helpful to you and Mrs. Reynolds—"

"You think you shall be spared their energies!" She covered her mouth. Unladylike guffaws escaped despite the effort. "Do you believe all our preparations will exhaust them? I must disabuse you of the notion immediately. While they might, at times, make themselves useful in modest ways, the dinners and parties will send them into fits of raptures only to be resolved by trips to the modiste, and linen drapers, and—"

"So they will require new dresses." He shrugged. "That insures your mother will approve the invitation."

"You will be fortunate if my mother does not decide to come to chaperone Kitty herself."

His eyes bulged.

She pulled his face close and kissed him. "I should not tease you. Given Kitty's letters, I do not think Mama is in any spirits to travel."

He met her gaze and looked straight through to her heart. He always understood.

"Are you disappointed?" His fingers grazed her cheek.

"No…well, perhaps a little. She does host excellent parties—"

"I am sure yours will be equally delightful."

"At least we will enjoy plenty of pleasing company. Mary and Mr. Pierce and Mr. Bradley will be here at least as often as they are at the parsonage." Elizabeth glanced out the window overlooking the path to the parsonage.

"Your sister and Pierce have been good for Bradley. I do not ever remember him so content, or comfortable. Though he rarely allowed me to call the apothecary to tend his ailments, he seems quite happy to allow Mary's ministrations. I cannot believe how much your sister has blossomed caring for Kympton parish."

"I am as proud of her as you must be of your cousin Richard."

Darcy brushed a stray curl off her forehead. "I despaired that he would ever establish himself outside the army. Jane's influence has settled him like none other."

"It would appear we Bennet girls work a world of good wherever we go." She kissed his cheek.

"Yes, you do. I suppose Pemberley will have more good than it is able to bear with all your sisters gathered for Christmastide. I nearly forgot. Bingley's letter arrived yesterday. He accepted our invitation as well."

Elizabeth sat up and folded her hands tightly in her lap. "What a lovely thing for our sisters—"

He rolled his eyes and pinched his temples. "You look and sound precisely like your mother."

She laughed into his shoulder.

"You teasing woman!"

"Of course, it is the best tonic for your disposition. Now, release me from this delightful position so I may...*we* may both resume our less frivolous pursuits. I have an entire Christmastide for our friends and family to plan." She kissed him and rose.

He handed her the stack of letters. "Thank you."

She took them and returned to her desk. Mr. Bingley would be here for the holidays. Was Darcy aware of the *tendre'* between his friend and her sister? She peeked at him. If he was, he gave no sign. Besides, he abhorred matchmaking.

Kitty would be happy to renew her acquaintance with Mr. Bingley, assuming that he had not found another young woman to admire. For all her sweetness, Kitty's jealous streak could make the house party uncomfortable at best.

Then again, the possibility for awkwardness existed in any house party. Best not dwell on it. Hopefully, Kitty and Georgiana would get on well together. When Elizabeth had left Georgiana in

London, she was still struggling with Lady Matlock's improvements. Perhaps her new companion, Mrs. Hartwell, would enjoy better success.

She trimmed a sheet of foolscap with her penknife, smoothed it in front of her and dipped her pen. *Dear Papa…*

❧ Chapter 2

December 21, 1811

A FEW MORE STITCHES, and the embroidery on the bodice would be done. Kitty examined the hoop of pale yellow muslin in the morning light. Drat! Several tiny stitches fell wrong, yet again.

A soft rap on the door demanded her attention.

"Miss Bennet?" Hill poked her head in. "The mumpers are coming up the lane."

"St. Thomas Day already?" Kitty dropped her tambour and hook and hurried to the window. A small group of old women wearing faded, patched gowns and ragged shawls tottered toward the house. "Why do they come so early?"

Hill peeked over Kitty's shoulder and shrugged. "They must start early if they are to call upon all the better houses of the neighborhood. They cannot walk nearly so fast as they used to."

Kitty returned to her chair and picked up her work.

"Please, Miss. I do not think the mistress is ready for company now, but I am sure she would want Longbourn to greet them properly."

But it was Mama's job, not hers! Kitty barely contained her huff. Hill always scolded when she huffed. "Yes, yes, of course. I will be down presently."

Hill dipped in a stiff curtsey and disappeared.

Would that Hill would stay away and keep her temper to herself. At least she had not yet begun to rail. Small blessing, still—Kitty smoothed her crisp lawn skirt and drew a deep breath. Would Mama ever stop being indisposed all the time?

When Jane and Lizzy were at home, they stepped into Mama's role at times like this. Now that she was the only sister at Longbourn, all the disagreeable duties fell to her. As usual, Lydia managed to leave her with all the unpleasantries whilst she escaped to have fun.

Coarse voices filtered from the kitchen. Bother, they were already inside! If she did not hurry, Hill would come after her again, ringing her a fine peal all the way. Why did all old women sound so raspy and nasal and horrible? She quickened her pace.

Kitty opened the kitchen door and nearly crashed into Mrs. Black. The toothless widow hunched over her cane, her balance so unsteady any breeze might topple her. She swayed dangerously.

"Excuse me!" Kitty grabbed the old woman's elbow.

"Not to worry, Missy Bennet. If you would, just give a body a bit of a hand." She leaned hard into Kitty's grasp and wavered several more times and came to rest. She tapped her staff on the floor three times. "There now, all be well."

Behind Mrs. Black, three more old women filled the kitchen with canes, dingy mobcaps, hunched backs and the odor of liniments brewed for oldsters' aches and pains. Each woman held a two–handled pot, newly scrubbed for the occasion.

The wheat! No! She screwed her eyes shut. She forgot to tell Cook—

"Tea is set in the morning room," Hill whispered. "Cook will fill their pots whilst you serve tea."

Kitty's eyes flew open and she threw her head back, sighing. Dear Hill! "Good morning. We...we are...very glad you have called." Could they hear her over her heart's drumming?

Why did Mama leave her all alone to do this? At least these old women seemed satisfied enough with her company—unlike the rest of Meryton. Of course, they could scarcely afford to be ungracious.

"Good morning, Miss Bennet."

Enough wool gathering! She twitched her head and sent the rambling thoughts away. "Would you join us for tea?"

Their clacking walking sticks and shuffling steps nettled her nerves like sand in her shoes.

The cream and roses paper-hanging in the morning room reflected the morning light. Sun beams glittered off the tea service set at the hostess's place. Plates of dainty sandwiches and biscuits, scones and dishes of homemade jams lined the center of the table, as fine a spread as Mama would use to entertain guests of quality.

"You are all so very, very good," Miss Yates intoned in a glass scratching voice. How was a woman, thin and frail as a wisp of muslin with gnarled tree-limb joints, in possession of a voice so grating?

"Longbourn is most kind to the likes of us, you know, when me and Miss Yates don't even live on Longbourn proper. So few concern themselves with the spinsters and widows these days..." Mrs. Black lifted a biscuit. Her trembling fingers scattered crumbs along the fine table cloth.

Spinsters and widows...Kitty nearly dropped the tea cup. Was that to be her fate? Who would marry her now when hardly anyone would even look at her? Perhaps an old widower would take her to manage his children and house. Such a man would never love her. She clutched the tea cup so tightly her hand shook like Mrs. Black's. No one would ever love her.

"What is this?" Papa's bristly voice announced his arrival. His wrinkled green coat hinted that he had fallen asleep fully dressed, again.

"We come a'thomasing, Mr. Bennet, sir." Mrs. Black crooked her neck to peer up at him. Her eerie toothless grin drove another pang deep into Kitty's gut.

"And we be offering blessings and good will upon you and all your family." Miss Yates rose shakily.

The other women followed suit. One reached into her dirty, striped market bag and produced a small lace-trimmed sachet. From the scent, it contained lavender and something else Kitty did not recognize. Chamomile perhaps?

"For the mistress, sir."

Papa turned it over in his hands.

"I sewed, she dried the flowers. Miss Yates there did the fancy work and Mrs. Black made up the lace."

"Thank you. Mrs. Bennet will be very pleased." Papa peered over the rims of his glasses at Mrs. Black. "You make bobbin lace?"

"I do a bit, sir. I done much more in my younger days." She bobbed her head so hard she might fall over.

He nodded and slipped the sachet in his pocket. "Hill, send a tray to my bookroom. I will have a word with Mrs. Black before she leaves." He bowed from his shoulders. "Good day."

Kitty pressed her lips hard. Why did he not stay? Would it have been so very difficult?

The women turned expectant eyes on her.

Oh, dear—they must have some conversation, but what? What was it Mama did? Questions! She asked questions. Mama said that was the surest way to have conversation and set guests at ease.

So, Kitty asked after their children, their health, their homes and the weather. Perhaps too many, too quickly, but her queries filled the silence until tea was finished. She led them back to the kitchen where they received gifts of cooked wheat in their pots and small baskets of smoked meat and pickled vegetables. Crying more choruses of thanks, the mumpers left.

The kitchen door clattered shut. At long last they were gone and would not return until next St. Thomas' Day. She dashed upstairs and threw herself against her door. If only her strength alone might bar the fearsome thoughts from entering.

So meager a fortification stood little chance, and they filtered in, tightening their ribbon tendrils about her chest and throat. She would be as those mumpers—old and alone. She would have to rely on the charity of her neighbors when no one else cared for her.

And it was Lydia's fault.

She flung herself headlong onto her bed. The pillow muffled her wrenching sobs. Such was the mumpers' blessing.

⸺⸻⸺

Kitty shifted the basket on her arm. The streets of Meryton bustled with foot traffic, but no one stopped to speak to her. Several mothers, their daughters in tow, crossed the street or ducked into shops, no doubt to avoid contact with her. None looked at her or smiled in her direction. She might as well have been invisible.

She stared at her feet. Her hand-me-down nankeen half-boots, mud spattered and layered with road dust, needed a good cleaning. Since no one accepted her calls, and no one called on her, she would have plenty of time to attend to that task later this afternoon.

Her throat tightened hard around the lump she could not swallow back. She must not cry. How could Lydia have done this to her?

It was all so unfair! Lizzy and Jane and Mary, all married and immune to the effects of Lydia's folly, left her alone to bear it. She dragged her sleeve across burning eyes

Wait. Was that—yes, Charlotte and Maria Lucas, there, near the milliner's. Surely they would not cut her.

Kitty hurried across the street. "Charlotte, Maria! How good to see you!"

They curtsied.

"Had we known you were coming to town today, we might have walked together." Charlotte smiled as though Lydia's transgression never happened.

No wonder Lizzy considered her such a dear friend.

"Excuse me. I must nip in here for a moment." Maria pulled the shop door open and disappeared inside.

Not Maria, too! Kitty gulped hard and sniffled.

Charlotte took Kitty's elbow. "The coffee house is serving lemon creams. You cannot imagine how delicious they are with chocolate."

Kitty mumbled and nodded as she followed Charlotte down the street. She stooped to hide within her poke bonnet's generous brim. That is what they were for, was it not, to hide a young woman from the censure of society?

The dark walls, covered with too many decorations, invited them to find a place in the crowded coffee house. Conversations hummed around her. How could so many be smiling when misery enveloped her like a red riding cloak?

Charlotte left her at an out of the way table and procured a tasting plate. "I am sorry Maria did not join us. She does so enjoy sweets. I hope you did not think—"

Kitty flicked her hand and shook her head. "She is just doing as everyone else."

Charlotte pushed a plate heaped with cheery glasses of lemon cream, dainty slices of pound cake, savoy biscuits and shortcakes at her. "You simply must try the pound cake. I have never tasted the equal of it."

Kitty picked up a piece, examined it, and put it down again. She sighed. At least Charlotte would permit her the luxury of a little dissatisfaction.

Charlotte touched her hand. "You are still upset over Lydia?"

She blinked hard and turned her face aside.

"I understand," Charlotte whispered. "Maria's behavior has earned me no little censure."

Kitty gasped.

"It is true. The same families that cut you and your sisters this spring cut me as well." She stared at Kitty. "You did not know?"

"No."

"Before Lydia's...ahh..." Charlotte rubbed her palms together. "The Smiths, Longs and Bonds stopped keeping company with both our families."

"Indeed?"

"Lizzy and I discussed it."

"I was so busy sewing I never realized." Kitty worried the edge of the tablecloth between her fingers. "What did Maria do?"

"Maria is a thoughtless, foolish girl even as you saw just a few moments ago."

Kitty picked up the crystal glass of lemonade and sipped the slightly too sour mixture. She stared into the cloudy liquid. A few lemon pips swam along the surface. How like Charlotte to be so concerned for her feelings—not that it helped, but it was very sweet.

"I hope she will come to her senses soon."

"Even if she does not, I doubt she will ever rival Lydia." Kitty smoothed the tablecloth under her glass.

"Perhaps not."

Kitty crossed her arms over her chest. "I will never forgive her."

"I know you feel that way now—"

"I will always feel this way."

"Perhaps, perhaps not." Charlotte shrugged. "Have you spent much time with the Bonds? After Olivia—"

"No." Kitty snapped a biscuit in half. Pale crumbs littered the blue table linen. "The Bonds still blame Lydia for Olivia's elopement. You might think Margery Bond would be sympathetic. She has received as much censure as I. She said I am only getting what I deserve for being related to such a wicked girl." Kitty covered her face with her hands.

"What a horrible thing to say. Mrs. Bond certainly did not agree—"

"I do not know as I avoid her whenever possible. I cannot—"

"Perhaps you are taking this too hard."

"You do not understand."

Charlotte turned her face to the ceiling and shook her head. "It may be worth little, but you are always welcome at Lucas Lodge."

"Thank you. It is some comfort." Not that she actually felt any ease, but it was the right and proper thing to say. Kitty dabbed her eyes with the edge of her sleeve. How could she have forgotten a handkerchief?

"If you are so unhappy here, what about your aunt and uncle in London? Perhaps you might visit them for a month or two?"

"That is a good idea." Kitty nibbled the edge of her broken biscuit. "With four young children, my aunt would surely appreciate help. She does not employ a governess. I could make myself quite useful to her."

"I thought you did not like children." Charlotte's eyebrows climbed under the edges of her droopy bonnet.

Kitty huffed and crossed her arms. "Well, I shall learn to like them. At the very least, they will speak to me whilst no one here will."

Charlotte chuckled. "I am sure you will find your cousins delightful."

"I shall ask Papa for permission to write them. London is just a few hours away and the horses are not needed on the farm right now." She chewed her lip. "Do you think he might allow me to go?"

"I would not have suggested it if I thought it impossible or even unlikely."

Was it possible? Might she escape to a place where her disgrace was unknown? Surely the Gardiners would be willing, and Papa could not object if they did not. She blinked hard, her lips turning up just a mite.

The pound cake did look appealing. She took a hearty bite. "You are right. This is delicious."

Her heart pounded in time with her steps as she made her way home. Papa could be so difficult. Surely he did not expect she would behave as badly as Lydia. Would he deny her because of her sister? Please, let it not be so!

She pushed the front door open. If fortune shone on her, he would be in the parlor…but, no. Not only was the room empty, but the door to his book room was closed as well. She would not see him until dinner. A grumble roiled in her throat. He was never there when she needed him!

No use talking to Mama either. She had not left her room since Lydia's departure. Only Hill gained admittance. Little did Mama care for her only unmarried daughter!

Kitty swallowed hard and dashed upstairs. Jane and Lizzy's old sitting room was strewn with scraps of fabric and unfinished projects. Folded swatches of muslin and calico covered the window seat. Ribbons and lace draped the table. She fell into a worn blue brocade chair and dropped her basket on the floor. Had she ever been so entirely, achingly alone?

Even the Bingleys had abandoned her. Louisa's letters stopped with Lydia's departure. How did Louisa find out so quickly? Their place in society was fragile at best and needed protection. She did not blame them, but she missed them dreadfully.

Why did Jane or Lizzy or Mary not invite her along on their wedding trip? It was done all the time. A sister should accompany the new couple. Obviously, she was not good enough to be a companion to them now that they were important, married ladies. She pressed her fist to her mouth.

Now they were all far too caught up in their new responsibilities to be bothered with her. They probably all hated her now anyway. After all, was this not her own fault? Lizzy stopped one elopement; she had failed. If only she had seen it coming and intervened. If only—

Kitty swallowed back a cry, but it escaped nonetheless, a pathetic little kitten mewl. If her throat tightened any further, she might well stop breathing.

The room lost focus, and she blinked rapidly. Papa would never allow her to go to London. She would be trapped here in this horrid little town, languishing on the shelf forever.

She dropped her face into her hands. Now that they had been given permission, tears would not come. Vile things! Would nothing go her way?

Hill tapped her door for dinner. If her sisters had been home, she might have changed into a fresh gown. Papa probably would not remark if she arrived for dinner wearing her nightdress. He noticed so very little these days.

An empty dining room greeted her. How surprising. She sat in her usual place, the middle of the table. Though she might sit in Jane's or Lizzy's place, she did not. No, she could not fill their places. She would never be—

"Good evening." Papa sat down.

He wore the same green coat from this morning, new wrinkles evident on the back and elbows. Shadows shaded his eyes. Everything about him gave the impression of dusty, musty, old bed curtains hanging in a long unused guest room. He had not laughed in the months since her sisters left.

"Good evening, Papa." The words scraped her throat raw.

He carved the joint of mutton and placed a slice on her plate.

"Cook made your favorite tonight. I suggested Hill add roast mutton to the menu. It has been so long since we enjoyed it."

He nodded and grunted something unintelligible.

The hush in the room expanded, fought back by only the clinks of silver on china and the small noises of chewing. Such meager weapons had no hope of staying the oppression. It threatened to steal even her breath away. If she did not find courage to speak, she would suffocate in the smothering silence.

Papa coughed. His fork and knife clanked, loud as a church bell, as he laid them on his plate.

She jumped and gasped.

"I received a letter today that may interest you." He reached into his pocket.

Papa had not spoken so many words to her at one time since the night Lydia eloped. He unfolded a piece of paper, cross written with many lines.

Lizzy's hand! How long had it been since her last letter? What could she—

"You have been much on your sister's mind. She is concerned that Meryton might not be the best place for you now."

Her heart stopped a moment then and raced headlong. Dear Lizzy! Someone understood! "Oh yes! She is right. May I write to Aunt Gardiner and ask if they might allow me to visit—"

He held up his hand.

Hope tumbled to the ground and splintered into bitter little shards.

"I think not."

She jumped up. Her chair tipped backward. She caught it with her fingertips a hairsbreadth above the floor.

"Lizzy invites you to Pemberley for the whole of Christmastide, perhaps even through to February."

Her face tingled, and her ears rang. She turned toward him, though her feet remained rooted in place.

"Do you not desire to go? I am certain she will understand if you—"

Visit Lizzy? In Derbyshire? "No, no, I very much wish to go. I...I had not expected so generous an invitation."

"Especially considering your reception here."

She stared, slack-jawed, and clutched the back of her chair lest her knees give way.

"I will write her directly and inform her of your plans." He tucked the letter into his pocket.

"What are my plans?" She sank into her seat. "Will I travel by post?"

"Certainly not." His voice sliced the air with the precision of her shears.

"Sorry, Papa...I...I..."

He lifted his hand and scowled.

How did Lizzy tolerate that expression with such good humor? His mien was positively menacing.

"I can spare the farm horses for a day. I will accompany you to London myself."

"London? I do not understand."

"Miss Darcy and her companion are in London. You are to stay with them until Boxing Day. Then, you will go to Pemberley for Twelfth Night. What is more, you have been invited to join Miss Darcy for Christmas dinner with her Uncle, the Earl of Matlock."

"Do not tease me, Papa." She slapped her hand over her mouth. He did not like to be contradicted.

He passed her the letter. "Read it yourself. I do not jest."

Her hands trembled so hard she barely unfolded the paper without tearing it. She blinked until the blurry words cleared.

An invitation from a peer! Surely Lizzy and Jane's influence procured it, but she was invited. Poor Lydia, how envious she would be! She pressed her lips hard, though the corners of her lips still turned up.

"I take it you approve?" He smiled, but his eyes did not twinkle the way they used to.

"Oh, yes! I do, thank you."

"Very well then. You will leave in two days' time. Your sister already anticipated our response."

"Two days? I—"

"It is already settled."

"But I need—"

"You have gowns aplenty with all Lizzy and Jane left you. You may refresh one easily enough once you get to London."

He could not possibly expect her to attend an Earl in one of her sister's old gowns, but she dared not tempt her good fortune. Though agreeable now, he might well change his mind. Her shoulders sagged, and she ducked her chin. "Yes, Papa."

"That bit of news should have set your appetite to rights. Sit down, and eat your dinner. Your packing can wait."

She nodded and returned to her meal. Strange, the pease pudding she normally despised tasted entirely tolerable now.

Empty trunks lined the wall near the window seat of Jane and Lizzy's sitting room. Every surface held piles of garments and fabrics, shoes, hats and haberdashery. How would she ever decide what to bring?

Mama oversaw all Jane's packing, sorting out those things not fit for her new station. Mary endured Mama's assistance with good humor, though her patience was sorely tried. And Lizzy—she left nearly everything behind and her packing was done in a thrice. Now, Mama was nowhere to be found now. Clearly Kitty was not important enough to stir Mama from her melancholy.

She closed her eyes and pressed her temples. With no acquaintance in London, she had to make a good first impression. But what was necessary to accomplish such a feat? She wadded the pale yellow stockings with delicate clocking at the ankles and threw them across the room.

At least her sisters had not forgotten her. Lizzy's most recent letter promised a surprise from her, Jane and Mary would be waiting at Darcy House. Probably a book on ladylike deportment. Yet, with a dinner at an earl's house to anticipate, such a book might be a source of comfort.

Christmas dinner with an earl's family! What a wonderful opportunity to meet new people, people untouched by her disgrace! She hugged herself and twirled in the only empty spot in the room. What would a peer's house look like?

It would be very fine indeed, filled with elegant people, people who might befriend her. Perhaps she might even meet an eligible beau. It was entirely possible she would meet a man who would like her enough to be undeterred by her measly dowry. And his eyes would be blue, like Mr. Bingley's...

Her belly ached, and she shoved her fist in her mouth. Though she told herself over and over she did not like him any longer that did not make it true. She missed Mr. Bingley and his sister so desperately. Could any man be as pleasing as he? Would she ever find a friend as dear as Louisa?

She drew and released several deep breaths. Where was her list? By the bonnets? No—there under the pink spencer. She traced the hastily written lines with her fingertip, smudging the pencil marks. Bother, where was her pencil?

In her pocket, precisely where she left it. When had she become so addlepated? She crossed out several lines and wrote corrections beside. Yes, that would do. Papa would protest she brought too much, but her plans were so vague. What else could she do?

"Miss Kitty!"

When had Hill come in?

"The coach will be ready in an hour, and not one of your trunks is packed!"

"I will be ready on time. Here is the list of everything—"

Hill snatched the paper. "I see, I see. It still takes time to pack it all proper. Your father will be ever so cross."

Kitty snorted. Without anyone to help her, what did he expect?

"Mattie!" Hill cried from the doorway. "Get yourself here!" She turned to Kitty. "Between the three of us and your list, I believe we may just finish in time."

Hill was indeed correct. Packing took longer than she anticipated, but the last trunk shut as Papa rapped at the door.

"I am ready, Papa." Kitty panted.

"Take leave of your mother whilst your trunks are loaded."

Were they going to visit a solicitor for the reading of a will? His somber tone and glum features did not fit a pleasure trip to London. Best not remark, though. Lizzy might be permitted to tease. She would not. "Yes sir."

She followed him to Mama's room. He knocked on the door and pushed it open. She peeked in. Hill must have preceded them. Open curtains admitted bright morning sun that reflected off the apothecary's bottle, the constant companion on her bedside table., With all its pretty fabrics, pillows and lace, the room might have been cheerful, except for its occupant.

Mama lay propped in her bed, moaning softly as she stared at a ledger in her lap.

"Mama," Kitty whispered and minced a few steps closer.

"I am very ill today, very ill indeed." Mama tipped her face up. The lace edge of her cap drooped over her dull eyes, her voice threadbare, a scrap of muslin cut from a worn out gown.

"I know, and I am very sorry indeed." Kitty stood at the bedside and wrung her hands. Why could Mama not be happy for her?

"What do you want? I cannot bear you staring at me like that."

"I am...they are loading my trunks now...I will leave soon—"

Mama lost the little color left in her cheeks and tears filled her eyes. "Leave? Where? Where are you going? You are not eloping—"

Kitty grabbed her wrist. "No, no, Mama, I am not! Mama, please listen! I am to London with Papa."

"London? Whatever for?"

"To visit Miss Darcy. She will take me to Pemberley to stay with Lizzy."

"Stay with Lizzy?"

"Yes."

Mama's forehead knotted, and she blinked rapidly. Her chin creased with a burgeoning frown.

No! Mama could not forbid her to go, not now. Papa would not change his mind. Would he?

"Lizzy? Well, that...that is good. She will protect you. Mr. Darcy will keep you safe. He will not let you elope—"

"Mama! I am not—"

A heavy hand pressed her shoulder.

"Do not say it, Miss. It will only agitate her." Hill whispered, but her voice still boxed Kitty's ears.

How satisfying it would have been to stamp her feet and pump her fists, but behaving like Lydia never served her well. She swallowed hard. "I will be safe at Pemberley. Lizzy and Mary and Mr. Darcy and Mr. Pierce and Mr. Bradley will all be there to protect me"

"Mr. Bradley and Mr. Pierce, too?"

"Yes, and I will mind them all ever so well. I promise." She was not Lydia after all.

From the corner of her eye, she made out Hill's nod. Vexing woman!

Mama sat up a little straighter and offered a watery-eyed smile. "Of course, you will, of course. You are a good girl, and they will keep you safe."

"Good-bye, then. I shall write and tell you every little thing." She kissed Mama's cheek. When had her skin become sheer as the finest silk?

"The Master is waiting for you downstairs." Hill took her arms and propelled her toward the door so hard her feet caught along the carpet. "Dontcha be fearin' none, Miss. I will nurse her most faithfully. I hope she may be back to herself, maybe even by the time you return."

Kitty nodded. If she returned. Perhaps Lizzy or even Mary, or maybe Jane, might take pity upon her and allow her to stay with them for a very long time. She clasped the stair rail and paused. This might be the last time she ever descended these familiar stairs.

Chapter 3

SHE SQUIRMED ON THE SEAT. How different it was to travel without her sisters. They would squeeze into the coach, laughing and chattering. None minded the cramped quarters.

Cramped quarters with Mr. Bingley and Louisa would surely be a delight. They listened to her, attended to her stories, not trying to talk over her or hush her as Lydia did. Oh, to be traveling with them!

With Papa, she had no conversation at all. Traveling three hours in utter silence might well drive her to bedlam.

"So...Papa, will you return to Longbourn directly or have you business in London today?"

He shook his head sharply. "What? Oh, yes, I will stop to visit the Gardiners before I return. I expect to be back at Longbourn late tonight."

Curiosity prickled the back of her neck. Best she ignore it. As cross as he got at Lizzy for asking about his business travel, he surely would not be better pleased with her.

He wiped a smudge off the side glass with his sleeve.

She picked at her skirt. "I am glad I became acquainted with Miss Darcy when she visited for the wedding. I would be ever so nervous if I had not met her already."

Papa grunted.

She stared at him, fixed on the scenery outside. He was not going to talk with her, nor did he care to listen. No use fighting for his attentions. It was not as though she were accustomed to them anyway.

She opened her bag and pulled out pieces of dimity for a chemisette. It would look quite well with several of her gowns, and if she was quick, it might be completed by the time they arrived.

The sights and sounds of London rose up around them though her chemisette was still only half-finished. How had they reached their destination so fast? She turned to look through the rear glass, finding no trace of the countryside or Meryton. Her face tingled. Was there something in the London air that stifled her breath?

"Look there—I believe that is Darcy House." Papa pointed to a first rate townhouse faced in light color stone with simple, elegant appointments. She would have guessed it a Darcy property from the façade alone. The impressive structure, five windows across, made the Gardiner's second rate house look like a mumper's cottage.

"You are frightened?" Papa tapped the side glass.

"A bit intimidated perhaps." How would she manage not to humiliate herself? Simply not eloping would not to be enough.

"Will it be too much for you?"

Did he think her like Mama—wilting in the face of the first trial? Her cheeks grew cold, and she ground her teeth. "No. If Lizzy can manage, I can as well."

"You know the direction to your Aunt and Uncle's. Make sure you reserve enough money to hire a hack chaise should you need—"

"I will." She gulped.

The carriage stopped before the grand house. She clutched her bag. Providence gave her this opportunity to prove she was more Jane's and Lizzy's sister than Lydia's. She would succeed. She had to.

Her courage flagged at the door. Thank heavens Papa knocked. Her arms were too heavy to manage such a feat. Why did Lizzy's courage rise in such circumstances while hers was most apt to fail?

A somber butler admitted them, noting in a voice as formal as his livery, they were 'expected'.

Cool relief trickled into her belly. She had not truly thought they might be turned away, but in so grand a house, even the servants could see she did not belong.

The butler ushered them into a sunny parlor. Clearly the sunbeams were enchanted to be there. The simple, stylish furnishings provide a welcome play yard for the happy rays of sunlight that danced from the crystal to the mirrors and back again.

"The room looks like Lizzy," she whispered.

Papa nodded. The corners of his lips drifted up just enough to break the scowl had worn all the way from Longbourn.

Lizzy always made him smile. Kitty sighed softly.

"Miss Darcy, Mr. and Miss Bennet." The butler bowed.

What a pretty girl. Not beautiful, but pretty in a way other girls enjoyed, despite her envy-provoking fine, white gown. She wore a genuine smile with a hint of timidity. Perhaps they were very much alike after all.

Miss Darcy dismissed the butler with a nod. "I am pleased you are come. I trust your travels were pleasant. Please sit down. My companion, Mrs. Hartwell, will join us shortly. She is arranging tea."

"Thank you, I cannot stay. I have business to attend as I must I return to Longbourn tonight."

"Of course, I will not keep you. Would you stay long enough for the kitchen to arrange a hamper?"

Papa waved off the notion.

Kitty cocked her head at him. "That would be lovely. Papa hates to eat at public houses, and I doubt he will stay long enough at Uncle's to sup with them."

He pursed his lips and rolled his eyes.

Miss Darcy rang the bell. "We are most happy to send our hospitality with you."

"There is no need. I must—"

"The carriage is still being unloaded. We will not keep you any longer than necessary to unpack." She offered Kitty another timid smile. "Besides, I cannot have my sisters believe I would not show their father the best Darcy hospitality."

Papa heaved a deep breath. "As you will. I am grateful."

A quarter of an hour passed, and Papa was on his way. Kitty gripped the railing and waved at the coach. It would not do to run after it. A chill gripped her spine. Had she ever been without her sisters or some true family very nearby? Lizzy's courage would rise at a time like this, but Kitty did not trust her own.

A woman bearing a tea tray joined them in the parlor. Older than Jane and younger than Aunt Gardiner, her cheery print dress spoke of a station above mere servant.

"Miss Bennet, may I present my companion, Mrs. Hartwell."

They curtsied to one another. She was a prettyish sort of woman with Charlotte's practical bearing and an air of good sense. A hint of sadness lingered around her eyes.

"Tea, Miss Bennet?" Miss Darcy opened the lacquered tea caddy.

"Yes please." Kitty perched on a chair and clasped her hands tightly in her lap.

"You are likely to misshape your gloves if you wring your hands like that." Mrs. Hartwell said softly.

Kitty jumped and pulled her hands apart.

Miss Darcy shook her head, passed a tea cup to Kitty and glared at Mrs. Hartwell. "You will become accustomed to her soon enough. You can be certain whatever you do, Miss Hartwell will find some fault or another. She delights in being most forthcoming in letting you know."

Not at Darcy House one hour and already they found fault to correct! Kitty bit the inside of her cheeks.

Mrs. Hartwell folded her arms over her chest and flashed a Mary-like half-frown at Miss Darcy. "Mrs. Darcy hired me to assist you with all those small accomplishments and graces necessary to becoming—"

"A stuffy old society matron."

"A proper young lady who will bring credit to your family."

"Which I will when everyone notices what fine condition my gloves are in."

Mrs. Hartwell huffed and fluffed like a bossy hen.

"I never had a companion," Kitty whispered. "I will be grateful for your advice."

Miss Darcy handed Kitty a plate of biscuits. "Do not let her frighten you. She likes the role of strict governess a bit too well for my liking. Perhaps I should write my brother and tell him—"

"Oh do, please." Mrs. Hartwell sipped her tea. "He will certainly add a bonus to my pay if you do. He directed me to be as tyrannical as I wished and provide you with more direction than you might possibly follow.

Kitty's jaw hung open, and she stared from one to the other. Miss Darcy's attitude was so like Lydia. Even with Miss Darcy's station, a young lady needed guidance in proper behavior. This was Lizzy's choice of friend for her?

Miss Darcy collapsed into peals of laughter. "Please forgive me, Miss Bennet. I should not indulge in so much silliness—"

Mrs. Hartwell cleared her throat

"—but I have been without company for several months now and am perhaps a bit too merry. Be assured, I do refine my conduct in the company of my Aunt Matlock. She calls and issues invitations often enough." She glanced at Mrs. Hartwell, who drew herself up tall in her chair and pressed her hands into her lap, her elbows out like the wings of a scolding hen.

Kitty covered her mouth, but giggles still escaped. Why did Mrs. Hartwell not smile?

"Oh, you look just like her." Miss Darcy tittered.

"I was not aping your aunt."

Kitty squirmed. "My sister Jane—Mrs. Fitzwilliam now—is quite a talented mimic."

"My cousin's quiet, beautiful wife? Surely you must—"

"Oh, no, I am quite certain. She did it often enough at home."

"Now I know why I liked her so well."

"You have seen her recently?"

"She and my cousin left Matlock house last week. I expect we will see them at Pemberley. Richard—Colonel Fitzwilliam purchased an estate in Derbyshire, and they will stay at Pemberley until they take possession."

"How wonderful." Kitty clapped. "I had no idea that—"

Miss Darcy's hands flew to her mouth. "Oh dear! I think that was to be a secret."

Mrs. Hartwell glowered.

"I shall pretend I know nothing. I promise." Kitty pressed a finger to her lips.

Miss Darcy flashed a quick smile at her companion. "We will have a merry time together. I am sure of it. What other secrets can you tell me of my brother's and cousin's wives?"

A tiny wrinkle formed between Mrs. Hartwell's brows. Was it for her or Miss Darcy? She could not tell, and it became no clearer over the next several hours.

The housekeeper entered and asked for instructions regarding dinner.

"We will use the small dining room." Miss Darcy said.

"Very good, ma'am." The housekeeper curtsied and left.

"Oh! Oh! How could I forget? You must go upstairs to your room!" Miss Darcy sprang up and pulled Kitty to her feet.

"Where do you want me to go?"

Miss Darcy clapped her hand to her mouth. "Oh, forgive me! I am a dreadful hostess. We must show you to your room. Your trunks are already there. One of the maids will attend your gowns—perhaps she already has."

Miss Darcy led the way up the grand staircase, twice as wide as Longbourn's and half again as long. Mrs. Hartwell followed a step behind. The polished marble gleamed underfoot. A distinctive clatter echoed from her half boots while Miss Darcy's slippers whispered across almost silently. Kitty cringed. She sounded like a cart pony!

"Just down this hall." Miss Darcy grinned, barely containing a giggle.

Mrs. Hartwell opened an elegant oak door and revealed a beautiful room. Sleek and simple furniture stood out against the soft yellow walls. Blue brocade curtains hung at the window and on the bed, so like a picture in the Ladies' Magazine that she hardly noticed her trunks piled in the corner.

A long box, tied with a large blue ribbon fashioned into a perfect bow, lay in the center of the bed.

"Go on." Mrs. Hartwell gave her a little push. "Read the card."

Kitty's hands trembled as she struggled to free the card from the envelope. It was one of Lizzy's calling cards: *Mrs. Elizabeth Darcy* On the back: *For your dinner at Matlock House—Jane, Lizzy and Mary.*

Kitty squealed and released the bow. Folds of almost white but barely blue silk ebbed and flowed through the tissue paper. She floated her fingers over the surface.

"Show us!" Miss Darcy bounced on her toes. "It arrived from the modiste two days ago, and I have been ever so curious. Mrs. Hartwell would not let me peek."

Kitty lifted the silk reverently. Puffed sleeves frothed like a syllabub from the shoulder and pooled into a vandyke blue satin trim with tiny blue tassels dripping off the points. The skirt tumbled down and puddled in a generous train lined with matching trim, tiny bows in place of the tassels.

"For me?"

"You saw the card. It was made specifically for you. Do you like it?" Miss Darcy bit her lower lip.

"I have never seen anything so beautiful."

"I helped pick it out, you know."

"You did?"

"I wanted this fabric so much." Miss Darcy ran her hands down the skirt, "But I had just ordered a new gown, and my brother would not allow me another so soon." Her lips wrinkled into a dainty little pout.

"So you selflessly suggested it would make a lovely gown for one of your new sisters who might later permit you to wear it." Mrs. Hartwell's eyebrows rose into a high arch quite like Lizzy's did.

"I do not see what is so wrong with that. I chose the pattern according to what Elizabeth said *Miss Bennet* would like best. You remember, vandyke is *not* my favorite trim."

"I think it quite beautiful and very thoughtful. Why do you not try it on? Since you like it so well, you may be the very first to wear it."

"No, that would not be fair. It is your dress—" Mrs. Hartwell said.

She was right, but letting Miss Darcy try it on first would not make the dress a hand-me-down. Besides, giving happiness to her new sister could not be a bad thing, could it? Especially when they would be spending so much time together. "It would please me to see it on you."

"Really?"

"Yes. Let me undo your buttons."

Miss Darcy squealed and turned her back to Kitty, presenting a long row of tiny white buttons.

They helped Miss Darcy into the gown. She smoothed the skirt and twirled before the looking glass.

Kitty caught her bottom lip in her teeth. This was not a gown for a cart pony. "It is even more beautiful than I imagined. Are you certain?"

"Yes, your sisters ordered it expressly for you." Mrs. Hartwell crossed her arms firmly.

"Yes." Miss Darcy's shoulders slumped. "Vandykes are not my favorite trim."

"But I have no—"

"Not to worry." Miss Darcy changed into her own gown. "I have evening slippers you may borrow to wear with it." She dug into the box and found an envelope that she handed to Kitty. "My good and generous brother sent a gift as well. He said to take you to the milliner to purchase a bonnet to match the gown. He thought I should not choose everything for you."

The card in the envelope read just as Miss Darcy said and was accompanied by a five pound note. Kitty gasped.

"I told you he was generous."

"I did not expect—"

"Of course not! That is what makes this such fun. Shall we go shopping tomorrow? If you place an order, it might be finished for Christmas dinner."

"I always wanted to go shopping in London. Lydia will be so jealous when she finds out!"

"Lydia, your youngest sister? Why did Elizabeth not invite her, too? There is time yet. We can write to—"

Kitty winced. "Thank you. But she is…on a trip herself and unable to come."

"Oh? Elizabeth did not tell me. Where is she?"

"She is staying in the north for an extended visit." That was not a lie—not entirely.

"What a shame. We could be such a merry party."

Kitty forced a smile, the same one she wore since Lydia eloped. It felt so familiar now. Perhaps she lost the ability to smile genuinely. "Then I shall simply have to be merry enough for two."

Mrs. Hartwell gazed at her steadily. Her face betrayed no sentiment. She was eerily and implacably calm. What fault did she find now?

Kitty looked away.

"Please forgive me. I did not mean to suggest your company insufficient." Miss Darcy rolled her eyes. "I am so excited to finally have sisters. I suppose I am being greedy. After all, Elizabeth has Mary and soon Jane so near her."

Mrs. Hartwell grumbled. "You will be at Pemberley soon enough, and then you shall complain no one pays you sufficient attention."

"I will not."

"You might, once there are so many sisters about. It happened often enough at Longbourn." Kitty said. "You see—"

"Yes, Mrs. Hartwell." Miss Darcy frowned. "It does occur to me though, your dress is so exquisite, it does not match your name: Kitty. That is so plain and countrified a name. Since you are my sister now, I will call you...Catherine...yes, Catherine, instead—"

"I think not! You cannot dictate what people will be called as if they were your house servants. You may very well insist your maid always be called Hattie, but this is entirely disrespectful," Mrs. Hartwell snapped. "Please, Miss Bennet—"

"No, no, do not be alarmed. It is quite fine. My...my friend Maria Lucas said I should stop using Kitty if I want anyone to consider me a lady." Her voice wavered as her stomach fastened itself into a tight French knot.

Mrs. Hartwell touched Kitty's arm. "It was a rude and insensitive thing to say. You should ignore it entirely. You are Kitty, and she has no right—"

Kitty squared her shoulders and lifted her chin. "No, no. Miss Darcy is quite correct. I came to London for a change of scenery and to make that change complete, I think I should become Catherine." Could she be a Catherine, so royal, so elegant? Was it possible?

"You see, I was right. It is the perfect accessory for her lovely gown, and she can wear it all the time." Miss Darcy tossed her head the way Lydia did when she carried her point. "With her beautiful new name and you to coach her manners—"

A sour tang coated the back of Kitty's tongue, and her cheeks prickled. A new place obviously required a new name and new improved manners. If that is what it took to leave Lydia's stain behind, then she would do it.

"—she shall be the talk of Christmas dinner! I dare say, by the time Mrs. Hartwell is finished, any number of eligible young men will take notice of you, Catherine."

Mrs. Hartwell clutched her forehead. "That is entirely enough, Miss Darcy. I recommend you attend your own manners and the respectability of the Darcy name."

"We do not need to dwell upon unpleasantness, do we?" Miss Darcy's smile faded, and she blushed.

"Of course, we do. But we should allow Miss Bennet to prepare for dinner and discuss this privately." Mrs. Hartwell took Miss Darcy by the elbow and propelled her out the door. She gave Kitty a quick backward glance and shut the door.

Kitty collapsed on the bed. Would a Catherine do that? How close she had come to revealing her shameful secret? She must be more careful. If Miss Darcy found her manners unacceptable already, knowing the truth about Lydia would damage their relationship beyond repair. From now on, she had to make certain nothing of the old Kitty Bennet and her horrible sister remained.

❧ Chapter 4

KITTY SLEPT MUCH LATER than she did at Longbourn. Still, no voices or busyness greeted her as she venture out of her room. She stole downstairs, workbag swinging on her arm. The morning room should not be too difficult to find. Surely it must be near the dining room, probably on the east side of the house to catch the morning light. Daunting as she found the townhouse, what must the manor at Pemberley be like?

Poor Lizzy. Did Mr. Darcy call her that, or was she required to be Elizabeth to one and all now? Elizabeth and Catherine sounded well together, two very fine sisters entering into high society.

Sunlight poured from an open door. She peeked in. The morning room at last! She would enjoy this first morning as Catherine.

Mrs. Hartwell sat at the far side of the table, a book in one hand, a pencil in the other, and an open journal in front of her. "Good morning, Miss Bennet." She did not look up.

"Oh, forgive me! I did not mean to disturb you."

She removed her glasses and blinked at Kitty. "Not at all, please come in. The light is so favorable for fancy work." She pointed to the chair beside her, directly in a sunbeam.

"Thank you." Kitty slipped in and sat down. The light was ideal for the white on white embroidery she was working on the chemisette. Precisely the kind of work a Catherine would do. One loop, two loops, three and a tidy little knot—

"You are quite adept. Perhaps you might teach Miss Darcy. I have had no success instructing her."

"It is not so difficult. See, the trick is all in how the left hand holds the thread, not the right."

"I will keep that in mind. Though I think, perhaps, there is something to be said for the motivation of the stitcher as well. When you have always been able to pay someone else to do the disagreeable work for you, there is little reason to learn to do it yourself."

"But this is not at all disagreeable."

"For you."

"Oh." Kitty looked up.

Mrs. Hartwell returned to her book.

"If I may ask, what are you writing?"

"I am copying a receipt from the housekeeper's book. The cook uses it for her pickled cauliflower, and it is the best I ever tasted."

"My mother writes any number of ledgers. She keeps a very large book of receipts and housekeeping instructions, some written by her mother and grandmother. I love to see their handwriting. My grandmother penned her 'g's' the most peculiar way, like she never learnt to write them properly. I wonder if she said them oddly too."

"You read your mother's household book often?"

"My sisters—most of my sisters—and I study and copy from it regularly. Though I admit I skipped the receipts for pease pudding, as I cannot abide the stuff."

"I am not fond of the dish, either." Mrs. Hartwell chuckled. "Poor Miss Darcy has no such book."

"Her mother did not keep one?"

"I suspect she did, but I am not certain. Miss Darcy shows little interest in such matters."

Kitty stuck her needle into the dimity. "How sad. Perhaps she does not know what she is missing."

"Perhaps not. I cannot convince her, though."

"Have you been with Miss Darcy very long?"

"No, just a few months. Your sister insisted Miss Darcy needed a companion. She herself selected me for the position."

Kitty chewed her lip. "I am sure Lizzy—Mrs. Darcy—thought it ill-advised for Miss Darcy to be alone." Certainly she would after all that happened with Lydia!

"I am sure she did." Mrs. Harwell set her pencil down. "Miss Darcy is a good sort of girl. She had been given good principles, but I find concern in the way in which she follows them. There is something to be said for a more…practical upbringing. One may never predict what the future holds, and it is wise to be prepared."

"You sound like our friend Charlotte. Forgive me if I am too forward. You are a widow?"

"Yes. I should think that obvious."

"I…I…"

Mrs. Hartwell waved her hand. "Do not worry. I do not mind speaking of it. Eighteen months has dulled the ache, though I still must remember I am no longer in mourning when I dress each day." She closed the housekeeper's book. "He was something of a Jehu and could not resist a challenging drive. He borrowed money to purchase a high flyer phaeton, a break-neck cart really. Foolish vehicle by all accounts." She pinched her temples and shook her head. "He took his brother driving and became distracted by all the banter. The phaeton overturned. My husband died. His brother walked away."

"How awful."

"It was, but his brother helped me greatly."

"I expect so. He owed you as much, but how could you stand to be near him? Did you not—"

"Hate him? Blame him for the accident? Of course I did." Mrs. Hartwell shrugged. "But the grudge grew too heavy to carry."

"You forgave him?"

"I did."

"Why? How?"

"Why?" Mrs. Hartwell turned her face toward the window. "I decided to see if the vicar was right. He was. As to how, I do not think I am the one to ask. I must wake up each morning and choose to do it all over again. I persevere because, each time I do, I find peace."

"Peace enough to marry again?"

Mrs. Hartwell blushed. "How?"

"You are copying receipts into your own book. Why else would you need them?"

She bit her lip and smiled. "You are most observant."

"And he is—"

"A cousin, a widower, a clerk in a law office. He intends to purchase a practice soon. It is just a small one, but it will be enough to support a wife. His young daughter stays with his mother right now and he wants her to come home soon. It will be an advantageous arrangement for all of us."

What did one say upon learning of a servant's plans to abandon their position? "My uncle is a solicitor."

Mrs. Hartwell nodded. "You will not tell anyone?"

"I do not understand. I am sure Lizzy—"

"Because—" her voice caught, "you must appreciate that it is far easier to leave an excellent position than it is to find one. I had no a clear understanding with my cousin when I took the place here. I have no guarantees—I do not know when all may be ready for me to leave. I cannot risk being dismissed without another place to go."

"Is that not unfair to the Darcys?"

Mrs. Hartwell shook her head. "I do not think so. I am easily replaced. They stand to lose far less than I. A woman alone in the world must never forget her state, even with the most generous of employers."

"Of course." Her reasoning made sense. Still, could it be right to treat Lizzy and Mr. Darcy that way?

"Now you know my secret. Perhaps you will tell me yours."

"My what?" Kitty's cheeks prickled.

"It is clear something troubles you."

"Excuse me?"

"Forgive me if I am too forward or wrong altogether, but I think not. You carry a weight, a trouble with you."

"I…I…that is to say—"

"You need not say anything now. Just remember, if you desire a confidante, I am trustworthy with a secret."

"I…I will." However would she manage to hide who and what she was if Mrs. Hartwell saw through her so easily?

"Good morning, Catherine, Mrs. Hartwell." Miss Darcy stood in the doorway. "I suppose I am quite the lay-a-bed. You are both up and already so useful! Oh, how pretty! Do let me see what you are working on."

Kitty handed her the embroidery.

"This is exquisite. What are you going to do with it?"

"It is a chemisette for my day dresses."

Miss Darcy traced the pattern with her fingertip. "I am told my mother did this kind of work. I wish she had taught me."

"I have tried." Mrs. Hartwell frowned and glanced at Kitty.

"You are so impatient with me." Miss Darcy's lips pursed into a dainty pout.

That was easy enough to imagine. "Perhaps I might be able to teach you." She put the chemisette into her work bag.

"I would like that very much." Miss Darcy glared at her companion. "*She* is so particular!"

Kitty squirmed. Though she hated to agree, the self-same thought had crossed her mind.

After breakfast and a lengthy stay at the dressing table, Kitty met Miss Darcy in the foyer, and they followed Mrs. Hartwell to the waiting coach.

"Your carriage is lovely." Kitty settled into the soft squabs. "Our trip to Pemberley will be ever so comfortable. Do you know, at first, when Papa told me I was to go, I thought I might have to travel post." She giggled.

"Post?" Miss Darcy gasped. "My brother would never permit it! You cannot—"

"Not all families possess your brother's means. It would not be appropriate to assume he would provide an invitation *and* transport." Mrs. Hartwell glowered.

Kitty squirmed. Would her every word brand her a poor, ignorant country girl?

"Please excuse me, Catherine. I meant no offense." Miss Darcy blushed.

"None taken, I assure you." That was the right and proper thing to say. Was it not? Even if she did not feel it.

"Good! Now, where would you like to shop? We have the entire day. We can go to the Bond Street Bazaar or somewhere else I suppose."

Had Lizzy or Jane ever mentioned where they shopped? Yes! "Lizzy said something about a particular milliner on Bond Street."

"We will visit Mrs. Henri first." Miss Darcy settled into her seat. "I hoped you would choose her shop. We shall have such fun."

Mrs. Hartwell nodded. "I will instruct the driver."

The journey to Bond Street was a quick one—so easy a distance Kitty would have never thought to ask for the carriage. Perhaps one did not walk easy distances in London. She opened her mouth, the question poised on her lips. Miss Darcy raised an eyebrow, and she clamped her jaws shut.

The carriage slowed in a sea of city life. Odors from the busy street wafted in: horses and their waste; smoke—coal, wood and tobacco; cooking food of too many types to identify. More traffic than she had ever encountered jostled for space between the carriages and wagons. How did one breathe in such chaos?

Kitty clutched her skirts, crushing the muslin under her hands. So very many people: beggars in rags, little boys sporting skeleton suits; a dandy, dressed after the manner of Beau Brummel, stood on the corner. The lady on his arm might well have been a fashion plate from *La Belle Assemble.* They both dodged a clumsy shopkeeper in a ragged, dusty coat, arms piled high with boxes.

The carriage finally moved again, only to stop a moment later. The driver handed them out. Kitty gawked at a pair of young dandies who walked with an odd gait. What was wrong with them?

Oh! She must not stare at them, so she turned to the nearest shop window. Fine gloves, stoles and collars lined the display, all vying for her attention.

"Come!" Miss Darcy led the way next door.

Kitty barely tore her eyes away. Lydia, too, would drag her away from windows she longed to savor. Would it do much harm to spend a moment looking? Perhaps it was not elegant to gawp at shop windows, and Catherine needed to learn a new habit. She hurried after Miss Darcy.

A sign on the door read *Fine Millinery* in swooping gold letters. Kitty gulped and minced her way inside.

Heady French perfume mixed with the distinct aromas of wool, straw and feathers assailed her. Hat forms lined one wall. The adjacent one held racks of ribbon and lace, flowers, fruit and feathers. Fabrics, plain and exotic were tucked into shelves in the far corner. Those she understood. If only she could make her way to them—

"Miss Darcy!" A large-bosomed woman with a heavy accent, as much a part of her costume as her measuring tape and scissors dangling around her neck, rushed toward them. "How might I assist you?"

"Good morning, Madame Henri. I am in search of a hat—"

"I know just the thing. I received it from Paris only this week."

"Not for me, for my sister, Miss Catherine Bennet."

Mdm. Henri turned to the previously invisible Kitty. Her face fell slightly. "I would be most pleased to assist you, Miss Bennet." She curtsied, her knee almost touching the floor.

The back of Kitty's neck prickled. What was she to do with so many options! No doubt she would demonstrate herself an unpolished goose cap the moment she tried to select something.

"She is the new Mrs. Darcy's sister." Mrs. Hartwell murmured.

"Ahh! Of course! I see the resemblance." The milliner smiled a shop keep's smile, the one crafted to make a shopper feel revered and in the mood to spend. Kitty had seen it enough in Meryton. Apparently, shopkeepers were no different here.

How quickly the milliner's attitude had changed though. Such was the power of the Darcy name.

"Mrs. Darcy is a very beautiful woman, and her taste, exquisite! Are your preferences similar to hers?"

How kind of Lizzy to rescue her, even now. "Yes, they are...I am not entirely certain what I want...perhaps you might suggest something she would like—"

The large woman glanced at Mrs. Hartwell who nodded. "Have you a particular dress you seek to complement?"

Miss Darcy shouldered past Kitty and launched into a detailed description of the gown. Kitty tried to break in twice, but Miss Darcy had commissioned the gown and was much better able to describe it. Kitty stepped back and inched toward the wall of lace.

Oh, the Bucks point was exquisite! The Mechlin and Chantilly, so much finer that the ones in Meryton. And Honiton lace! No merchant in Meryton carried that. If only—

Miss Darcy dropped something on her head. "Do you like this? I think it will be lovely on you."

Kitty reached up and gingerly patted the...oh...a stovepipe bonnet. She grimaced.

"Miss Darcy, come. I found the new Indian shawls." Mrs. Hartwell beckoned her from the farthest corner of the shop.

"I love shawls!" Miss Darcy scampered away.

The milliner held up a mirror. "You do not like the shape?"

"Ah, well..."

Mdm. Henri removed it. "Your sister does not prefer that form either, though Miss Darcy tried to persuade her toward it as well."

Kitty released a deep breath.

"It is much too heavy for so light a figure as yours." She stared, turning her head this way and that. "I am thinking something much more delicate, a turban of sorts, with feathers, not too many—you are not a bird after all."

Kitty giggled.

"And…" she marched to the wall of trim. "Some of this."

A strip of the most beautiful Honiton lace! "Oh yes, please."

"Come let us see what can be done with these." The milliner picked up a handful of feathers in her free hand and led Kitty to a long table. In a few minutes, she had crafted them into a rough turban.

Kitty chewed her lip and reached for a scrap of braid and a strand of beads. She tucked them in and around the bits held in the milliner's strong fingers.

"The mademoiselle's taste is as fine as her sister's. Shall I fashion it up for you?"

"Yes, please do. I will need it for a Christmas dinner. Can that be done?"

"For one of the Darcys, absolutely." She tucked the model under the counter and wrote quick, cryptic notes in a nearby book.

"Are you finished so soon?" Miss Darcy peered over her shoulder.

Kitty jumped and gasped. What had she done wrong now?

"Tell me what you ordered."

No! Miss Darcy would surely criticize and force her to change her design. But perhaps Miss Darcy knew better—

"How much more fun to keep it a secret, and be surprised when she shows it to you together with the dress?" Mrs. Hartwell said over Miss Darcy's shoulder

"I…I…"

"You are just like your sister." Miss Darcy huffed and folded her arms. "Must you spoil my fun?"

Kitty grabbed the edge of the counter, lightheaded. She was behaving as Lizzy? Then, she was doing well indeed. "I am not spoiling it. The fun is in the anticipation. It is the way of sisters to do these things, you know."

"I am not sure I like it very well."

"Perhaps now would be a good time to stop for a cup of chocolate?" Mrs. Hartwell stepped between them.

"Do you like chocolate, Catherine? Or will you keep me in suspense over that as well?" Miss Darcy's lower lip extended slightly, though not enough to draw Mrs. Hartwell's ire.

Kitty looped her arm in Miss Darcy's. "I do like chocolate and am most anxious to taste whatever you recommend."

"My favorite chocolate house is nearby. They serve the best by far." Miss Darcy led them out.

✥ Chapter 5

A LARGE SIGN PAINTED with a blue china cup hung above the chocolate house's door. Kitty rushed inside and dropped into a seat, breathless and wide-eyed. How did one tolerate such a crush of people on the streets? Though Meryton had its poor, the small children begging so forcefully sent her diving behind Mrs. Hartwell's skirts. No wonder Mr. Darcy preferred the country. How did fine ladies become accustomed to this?

"I could sit here all day and drink in that fragrance." Miss Darcy drew a deep breath.

Kitty closed her eyes and savored the exotic spices woven amongst the whiffs of chocolate, tobacco and coffee. They hung in the air and draped in great cascading folds over the bare ceiling rafters. She could almost imagine herself somewhere quiet and peaceful.

"Have you a chocolate house in Meryton?"

"The coffee house serves chocolate, too. I rather like the scent of coffee and chocolate together." Kitty bit her lip. Was that an ignorant thing to say?

"I do as well." Mrs. Hartwell smiled.

A young woman, in a white apron dotted with drops of chocolate and splashes of coffee tied over a drab dress, took their order and scurried off. Cheery, well-dressed people filled almost every table, and none stared with thinly veiled disapproval or whispered behind their hands whilst looking at her. London did have its virtues.

"I brought my friend Miss Lackley here whilst we visited my aunt, and she declared it the best chocolate. She has returned to Derbyshire now, but I will introduce you to her when we get there. You will like her ever so well. She is very pretty and keeps house for her brother. Mr. Lackley is a fine gentleman—"

"Miss Darcy? Miss Bennet?"

Kitty jumped and turned. It was not possible—that voice!

"Mr. Bingley!" Miss Darcy rose.

Kitty followed suit and managed a curtsey without falling over. It was awkward and not worthy of a Catherine, but she could manage nothing better whilst her heart raced and face flushed to the point of dizziness.

"Mr. Bingley, may I introduce my companion, Mrs. Hartwell?"

He bowed so gracefully, he might have been on the dance floor.

"Do sit with us, Mr. Bingley. My brother would insist." Miss Darcy sat down with a great show of smoothing her skirts.

"What a pleasant surprise to see all of you." His smile had not changed at all!

He looked at her, blue eyes twinkling and warm as ever. Did he still wish for her acquaintance?

It had been Louisa who stopped writing, after all. So it was possible. Her face tingled, and she lost all power of speech.

Miss Darcy cleared her throat. "I did not know you were in London, Mr. Bingley. I wish my brother would have told me."

Mr. Bingley still had that odd little curl, just so, over his forehead and the single dimple in his left cheek. The crinkles beside his eyes remained unaltered, as did the tiny mark on his left earlobe.

Mrs. Hartwell cocked her head, eyebrows creeping to meet the lace on her cap.

Oh dear, she had been staring. Best she say something soon. But what? "Your sisters, sir, are they well?"

"My sisters?" His cheeks darkened and he tugged the edge of his collar. "Caroline—she is much as she ever was. She continues with our aunt in Scarborough." He squeezed his eyes shut for the briefest of moments.

"And Louisa?"

He released his collar and the creases left his forehead. "Hurst's sisters invited her to stay with them. He should arrive from the continent at the end of next month."

"I trust her visit a pleasant one."

"Indeed. She is so pleased in their company she has barely written me. I think I have received but one letter from her. You know what a diligent correspondent she usually is." He chuckled.

Kitty laughed because he did. Louisa had not written him either? She clutched the edge of the tablecloth.

He blinked at her.

She must respond! "Mr. Hurst is to return next month? How wonderful for her. I recall she thought it would be much longer. Have they decided on a wedding date?"

Miss Darcy twitched like Lydia left out of a conversation. But what did she expect? It was only polite for Kitty to ask. Was it not?

"Mr. Hurst is my sister's betrothed. He has been away on the continent for business."

"I see. I did not know you knew Mr. Bingley or his sisters, Catherine." Miss Darcy's voice took on a thin, sharp edge.

Mr. Bingley stared at Kitty, brow drawn.

"I had not thought to tell you. We all met in Meryton. Do you not remember? Louisa was at the wedding. Miss Caroline—"

Mr. Bingley winced.

"—was already in Scarborough by then and was...unable to return for the wedding." Not that anyone minded Miss Caroline's absence. Kitty peeked at Mr. Bingley who closed his eyes and nodded.

"So will you go to Scarborough for the holidays?" Miss Darcy asked.

"No—"

Kitty gasped. "You will be alone?"

"Actually, Darcy invited me to Pemberley for Christmastide."

Kitty's jaw dropped in what must have been a most unladylike expression, but she could not force it closed.

"Yes." He reached into his pocket, his smile brighter and broader. "In fact, I called at Darcy House earlier this morning—"

The girl arrived, laden with a chocolate pot, cups and a plate of miniature gooseberry tarts. "I took the liberty of bringing an extra cup, Miss, seein' the gentleman here with you." She curtsied.

Miss Darcy glanced at Mr. Bingley and batted her eyes.

Mr. Bingley pulled back slightly and looked at Kitty "Ah...yes...thank you. I should enjoy that."

Did Miss Darcy have an interest Mr. Bingley? What was the nature of their acquaintance? Why had he come to join them?

The girl placed the pot on the table. She grabbed the chocolate mill and spun it furiously between her palms. Hot perfume rose from the chocolate pot, traces of cinnamon, nutmeg and anise wove into a heady blend. She poured four cups, each topped with a head of bubbling froth.

"Oh, yes. I was saying I left my card since you were not at home." Mr. Bingley glanced at the paper in his hand as though he had forgotten why it was there. "Darcy wrote me and suggested we might make the trip together. Mrs. Darcy is concerned with her sisters journeying alone, even in the presence of the formidable Darcy footmen." He chuckled. "He suggested, Mrs. Hartwell, you might wish to see the request in his own hand." He passed the folded missive to her.

Mrs. Hartwell nodded as she read and handed the letter back. "Mr. Darcy is most solicitous toward us all. He sent me a letter, which came just this morning, alerting me to this possibility."

Miss Darcy's jaw dropped. "Truly?" She turned to Mr. Bingley. "You will journey with us to Pemberley?"

Mr. Bingley fixed his gaze on Kitty. "Darcy has asked me to."

Her cheeks heated. "I think we shall have a very pleasant journey."

"Indeed we shall!" Miss Darcy bounced. "I can hardly imagine pleasanter company for such a tedious trip."

Mr. Bingley turned his smile to Miss Darcy.

Kitty's chocolate lost its flavor.

After they finished their chocolate and tarts, Mr. Bingley excused himself, and Miss Darcy led them to several more of her favorite shops. As the hour decent young ladies ought to leave Bond Street approached, Kitty's feet weighed as much as the parcels they had purchased. Thank heavens for the carriage.

"What a wonderful day." Miss Darcy threw her head back into the squabs. "Shopping with a sister is ever so much better than shopping with a brother."

"I am utterly exhausted." Kitty said.

"You cannot disagree, though. We have had a most productive day of it—you ordered your hat, which I will get you to tell me of yet." Miss Darcy laughed. "And I found that dear little muff and tippet. Best of all, we had the company of the charming Mr. Bingley! Imagine it! He will accompany us to Derbyshire!"

Kitty felt Mrs. Hartwell's penetrating gaze, but refused to meet it. Lizzy must have appointed her as Miss Darcy's companion on the basis of that trait alone. Kitty squirmed and cleared her throat. "It is most agreeable."

"Agreeable? That is all you can say?" Miss Darcy slapped the seat beside her.

"It is most considerate of him and Mr. Darcy—"

"Agreeable and considerate? A most handsome and eligible man will be in our company for three entire days, and you call it only pleasant—as though your pet dog were riding along?"

"You…you think him handsome?"

"Handsome, well mannered, charming, and he is my brother's friend, so he must be acceptable."

Kitty gripped the seat cushions. Shaking the dreamy expression off Miss Darcy's face would be most un-Catherine-like. "Acceptable for what?"

"He would make a very acceptable beau, do you not agree?"

"Miss Darcy!" The edge on Mrs. Hartwell's voice could have sliced through the thickest buckskin like newly sharpened scissors.

Kitty jumped.

Miss Darcy braced her hands on the seat and opened her mouth.

"You are not out and will not be for another year, quite possibly two. A girl who is not out cannot have a beau, nor should she be thinking about them."

"But Mr. Bingley is my brother's friend. He is different." Miss Darcy leaned forward. "Why else would my brother have suggested he travel with us? Besides, *you* let him join us for chocolate."

"You were permitted his company at the chocolate house because he is Mr. Darcy's friend *and* Miss Bennet's acquaintance. No other reason. You are not out—"

Her shoulders fell, and she hung her head. "I know, I know. You never let me forget. I still do not see—"

"That is exactly why you are not out and why, I might remind you, you spent the last several months under your aunt's tutelage."

"We do not need to discuss that in front of…anyone else." Miss Darcy sniffled.

Tension rose, thick as one of Cook's lumpy gravies and nearly as palatable, too. Could she find her way back to Darcy House on foot?

"Is Catherine out?"

The coach was moving a bit too fast for her to jump from it now. Still, it might be better than being caught between them.

"According to Mrs. Darcy, she is." Mrs. Hartwell nodded toward her.

Kitty dodged eye contact.

"That is not fair! Rebecca is out. My cousin is out. Catherine is out—everyone but me is out."

"All the girls you name are older than you by two years at least."

"But, but…I should be out, too! I am sure Catherine does not agree with all your restrictions." Miss Darcy turned expectant eyes on Kitty. "You do not want me to miss out on all the fun. Do you?"

Had Lydia suddenly appeared in the coach? Kitty's mouth went dry. "I…I can see the wisdom in waiting to be out. Too much company can be a highly overrated pleasure. With all the demands of fashion and fear of gossip, not being out seems an attractive prospect."

Miss Darcy bounced on her seat and crossed her arms over her chest.

"I expected you to have learned better from Lady Matlock by now. She and Mr. Darcy will be most disappointed when I tell them—"

"Tell them? No, you cannot."

"It is what I have been employed to do."

"Please, no. I did not mean it. I am…disappointed. Surely you understand. I like Mr. Bingley and I—"

"I see what you would like. However—"

"—until I am out, I must not think about liking any man." Miss Darcy hung her head and folded her hands.

"And?"

"And I must concentrate upon improving myself, so I will be a credit to myself and my family when I am permitted in company."

"Be certain you keep it in mind."

"Yes, Mrs. Hartwell."

"It is not so bad," Kitty murmured.

"How would you know? You are not the one who is not out when everyone else is."

"But all my sisters are already married, and I am the only one left at home."

Miss Darcy sighed. "I suppose that is very difficult too."

At the town house Miss Darcy claimed a headache and retreated to her rooms. Mrs. Hartwell suggested Kitty might like to rest a bit before dinner. Would that she could hide the remainder of the evening!

Had Miss Darcy set her cap for Mr. Bingley? Kitty swallowed hard, lest she cast up her accounts. Worse still, Mr. Bingley appeared to like Miss Darcy, too. After all, *she* was the one whom he addressed first at the chocolate house. He smiled at *her*, seemed very pleased in *her* company.

Why would he not like Miss Darcy better? She possessed a generous dowry, her brother was his greatest friend, and she had no foolish younger sister who ruined her family's reputation. Miss Darcy was a brilliant match, while neither Kitty—nor Catherine— had anything to offer. The sooner she forgot about him, the better it would be. She wrapped her arms around her waist and rocked against the bedpost. London was an awful place indeed.

Who was tapping at her door?

Mrs. Hartwell peeked in. "Would you join me for dinner in my sitting room? Miss Darcy is taking dinner in her rooms. I find even the small dining room a bit overwhelming for only two."

"It is very large." Kitty stood and shook out her skirts. Self-pity was unbecoming for a Catherine. "It would be lovely to eat with you."

"I already asked the housekeeper to send it up." Mrs. Hartwell smiled and motioned for her to follow.

The hall, easily twice as wide as Longbourn's, continued on so long Kitty feared they might be lost. On the verge of giving up hope they would ever arrive, they stopped and Mrs. Hartwell opened a door.

The sitting room was snug and pretty and finer than any room in Longbourn. Sprigs of pink roses dotted the paper-hanging and peeked out around the dark, elegant furniture. A small table held dinner.

"The staff here are very efficient, are they not?" Mrs. Hartwell sat at the far side of the table. "It can be a bit unnerving when one is accustomed to doing more for oneself."

Kitty placed the napkin on her lap. "I am glad not to be the only one somewhat ill-at-ease."

"Oh, I did not say that." She scooped roasted potatoes onto her plate. "At first I was. I supposed I should be embarrassed by how easily one becomes accustomed to excellent service. I expect I shall miss it when I finally do leave."

"Is it not enticement enough to stay with the Darcy family?"

"As fine a family as they are and as easy as my terms are, nothing is as desirable as a home of one's own."

Why did she not feel more loyalty to Lizzy? Though Mama could be a difficult mistress, no servant at Longbourn would say such things, would they? Hill surely would not.

They ate in silence for several minutes.

"How are you acquainted with Mr. Bingley? I know he is a friend of the Darcys," Mrs. Hartwell asked.

"He leased a home near ours for a short time during the spring."

Mrs. Hartwell cocked her head. "Come now, there is far more to the story. Your downcast eyes and quiet demeanor suggest a tale of intrigue and suspense worthy of a gothic novel."

"No, it was not nearly so exciting."

"But there were points of interest?"

"Yes."

"Tell me."

Mrs. Hartwell would not be gainsaid, so Kitty related the tale to make the most of her friendship with Louisa and the least of her relationship Mr. Bingley.

"I have always been afraid of fires." Mrs. Hartwell shuddered. "I cannot imagine how you talk of it so calmly."

"It was awfully frightening, but the gentlemen were so gallant. A novel's hero could not have been more valiant."

"Was Mr. Bingley among those heroes?"

Kitty blushed and turned aside.

"He certainly seemed pleased to see you today."

What would *Catherine* say? "I am certain he was pleased to see Miss Darcy. He is quite amiable."

"Perhaps."

Kitty squirmed, and bit her tongue. She did not have four sisters to be unable to keep her counsel.

"He asked permission to call at Darcy House tomorrow."

Kitty looked up. "I am sure he would like to discuss the details of the journey to Derbyshire."

"You would not enjoy his visit?"

"I did not say that. He is most pleasing company."

Mrs. Hartwell nodded and finished her meal.

How was it her silence felt as pointed as her questions?

The maid came to clear the table.

"So how did you find the stewed oysters on toast?" Mrs. Hartwell pushed back from the table just a mite.

"Mama never served them. She deemed them too inexpensive to grace Longbourn's table."

"What a shame, I find them quite tasty."

"But the texture—"

Mrs. Hartwell threw her head back and laughed. "Mrs. Darcy said the self-same thing whilst she was here."

"How long did Lizzy stay?"

"As I understand, they arrived a month or so after the wedding and stayed a month, during which time I was hired. I shared the house with her for a fortnight."

"Miss Darcy stayed in Darcy House alone before then?"

"No, she visited with Lady Matlock."

Kitty rubbed her knuckles along her lips. What would it be like—staying with a peer and having a countess guide your accomplishments?

"Do you wonder why Miss Darcy did not accompany them back to Pemberley, especially when Mrs. Darcy is so accustomed to the presence of sisters in the house?"

"I am sure Miss Darcy wished to stay longer to enjoy the company of her aunt and cousin and the diversions of London." Kitty shrugged.

Lizzy had written Kitty's invitation in her own hand. Surely Lizzy had not become opposed to the presence of a younger sister.

"You are gracious and determined to think the best of everyone. Many would benefit from your philosophy, including Miss Darcy herself."

"You do not approve of her?"

"It is not for me to approve or disapprove."

Kitty blushed. "Forgive me. That was not an appropriate question."

"You misunderstand me, Miss Bennet. I was not hired to pass judgment upon her, but rather to improve her character."

"Lizzy said that?"

"Both Mr. and Mrs. Darcy were quite clear in their instructions."

Kitty chewed the inside of her cheek. "I am certain I have a great deal to learn whilst I am here."

"That may be true."

Of course, it was. Kitty clasped her hands tightly under the table.

"I have, though, received no instructions regarding your education. Those who recognize their own need for improvement rarely need to be pushed to find it. For those who do not, however, the path is far more challenging."

"Miss Darcy?"

Mrs. Hartwell nodded. "Mr. Darcy sent her to Lady Matlock. He hoped the countess might affect certain improvements in her character during her stay."

"He was not satisfied in her progress when he visited?"

"Nor was Mrs. Darcy. She suggested a firm companion and the absence of amiable company might be more effective. You are Miss Darcy's first company in three months now. I am not impressed with her response, nor are you, I imagine."

Kitty shrugged and looked away. "I am not fit to speak on that matter."

"A fair and well-spoken answer, but not everyone will be so gracious with her. She risks disgracing her family if she continues as she is. It is my job to try to prevent that eventuality." Mrs. Hartwell laced her fingers in front of her chest. "May I count on your assistance with Miss Darcy?"

"What assistance can I provide? I am not—"

"You are a young lady concerned with improving herself. She would do well to emulate you."

Kitty turned and stared. "Me?"

"I believe your sister had that in mind when she suggested you visit."

Hours later, Kitty sat in the window seat of her room. The moonlight toyed with shadows in the garden below. Something small—a rabbit perhaps— scampered across the ground and under a bush. She envied the creature its freedom to run and hide from all things frightening or troublesome.

What had Miss Darcy done that Lizzy and Mr. Darcy would send her away? Kitty chewed her knuckle. Would they send her away too if she disappointed them? Mrs. Hartwell praised her and seemed to think her a good influence, but then Mrs. Hartwell did not know what Kitty had left in Meryton.

Her stomach churned. Nothing would ever change the stain she bore. How foolish to believe simply leaving Meryton would remove Lydia's disgrace. Mrs. Hartwell's praise meant little when others would only see her shame.

Worse still, Mr. Bingley. Clearly Miss Darcy liked him. What hope had even Catherine of keeping his regard in the presence of Miss Darcy, even if she was not out? She was young and pretty and in possession of a dowry fit to catch any man's attention.

Kitty's—and Catherine's—hopes dissolved into tears and dripped down her cheeks.

❧ Chapter 6

Sunrise stole into her room and teased her awake. She tried to hide under the counterpane, but it stole through the cover, tormenting, until she opened her eyes and surrendered. Botheration! She must remember to close the curtains at night. Perhaps if she closed them now—

She stole to the window and peeked out. Street sweepers already attacked the streets with their brooms. Carts loaded with goods trundled past. Doubtless the staff was already busy as they would have been at Longbourn. No use returning to bed. A fall-front day dress that required no assistance from a maid and a simple bun in her hair would do for the day. She crept downstairs.

It was Christmas Eve. At home, she and her sisters—no wait, no one would be there to go out to cut evergreen and holly boughs for decorating the house. She stopped and sank down to the stair step, face in her hands. All those things she used to do with her sisters were over, and she might now be alone, forever.

The scent of cut boughs tickled the edges of her imagination, so real she might reach forth and stroke the needles.

"Oh, Miss!"

She gasped and jumped up. A young maid stood two steps below, her eyes very wide. "I am sorry Miss—a delivery just come for you downstairs."

Kitty followed her into the foyer. A pile of evergreen boughs, a bunch of holly branches and a clump of mistletoe lay against the wall. The housekeeper appeared and handed her a card.

She opened it. We will miss gathering greens with you this year. When you arrive, we can collect more if you like. But for now, these will have to do.~Lizzy

Kitty forced back the lump in her throat. Her sisters, the older ones at least, were all that was good and kind and thoughtful. Even if she did not marry, there would still be those who cared about her.

"Are you pleased?" Miss Darcy peeked over the housekeeper's shoulder.

"Pleased and very surprised." Kitty knelt beside the evergreens and pressed her face into the needles.

The fragrance embraced her. She could almost hear the happy echoes of Christmas Eve at Longbourn.

Miss Darcy clapped softly. "I am so happy. It was dreadful difficult to keep the secret."

"Secret?"

"Yes, Mrs. Darcy made the arrangements as soon as she invited you to come." Mrs. Hartwell stepped around Miss Darcy.

"Just this morning, I was pining for the times we would go out in my father's woods to cut these."

"The woods at Pemberley have evergreen and holly aplenty and hellebore, too."

"Oh, I love Christmas roses."

"We shall have to look for some when we get there." Miss Darcy clapped softly.

"Shall we hang these?" Mrs. Hartwell lifted a branch.

Miss Darcy gathered several small branches. "Oh yes, let us do. Though first we must save some for a kissing bough."

"A what?" Mrs. Hartwell frowned.

"A kissing bough. Have you ever made one, Miss Bennet?"

"Mama insisted we fashion one each year. I often caught my father stealing kisses from her below it. My sisters and I would take turns keeping watch and counting how many berries he plucked himself."

"I never thought of a husband stealing kisses from his wife. What a novel idea. I wonder if my brother and—"

"That is not a proper thought for a young lady to consider." Mrs. Hartwell's tone sliced the air between them.

Kitty flinched. Catherine would not have told that story. Would she ever learn?

Miss Darcy sighed. "Is a kissing bough equally improper?"

"Since it is just us ladies here, and we are to depart in a few days, I find little harm in it."

Kitty bounced on her toes. "What fun!"

Kitty and Miss Darcy selected the best of the greens and mistletoe while Mrs. Hartwell dashed upstairs for ribbon. They met in the morning room, where the housekeeper waited with two wire hoops saved from kissing boughs from years gone by.

"You hold these together," Kitty placed the hoops in Miss Darcy's hands, "whilst we tie them."

It took them several tries and much laughter before the wire frames were secured into a sphere. They giggled and argued in the way of good-natured sisters as they trimmed and fastened boughs around the form.

"Apples! We must have some apples!" Miss Darcy disappeared for a moment and returned with a small bowl of bright fruit.

Fluffy bows attached the apples around the sphere and a cluster of mistletoe to the bottom.

"How beautiful!" Miss Darcy called for a footman to help them hang it near the parlor door.

Mrs. Hartwell stepped back and cocked her head to and fro. "I must say, that is much more attractive than I expected."

"She is not easy to please, is she?" Kitty tittered.

Miss Darcy stared up and twirled underneath the mistletoe. "No, she is not."

The door knocker's rap echoed through the front hall. The housekeeper hurried past and returned a moment later. "Are you home to Mr. Bingley and—"

"Yes, do show him in." Miss Darcy squealed and clapped softly. "We will invite him for refreshments. Have the kitchen send a tray."

Hot prickles crept across Kitty's cheeks. Mrs. Hartwell said he wished to call, but so soon? Had she only taken the time to dress properly! Perhaps she might run upstairs and change.

"Yes, Miss."

Miss Darcy stood under the kissing bough.

"Stop there."

Kitty stopped mid-step and looked over her shoulder.

Mrs. Hartwell glowered at Miss Darcy. "This is not why I granted you permission to make a kissing bough."

"What did I do?"

"You know very well, Miss Darcy."

"There is no harm—is that not what it is for? To stand under it?"

"You may wish to reconsider your attitude."

The housekeeper peeked in.

"You are determined to ruin all our fun." Miss Darcy waved her away. "Send Mr. Bingley away. I no longer desire company."

"No, he has already been shown in. Turning him away would be the height of bad manners. Take yourself upstairs. We need to have a long talk. Miss Bennet, would you mind acting as hostess?"

"Catherine gets to entertain our guest?"

"Yes. She knows how a lady is to behave."

"As do I." Miss Darcy stamped.

That must have hurt. Slippers did little to protect against the hard marble. Kitty blushed. Catherine would not know that.

"No, you do not." Mrs. Hartwell grabbed her arm and dragged her out.

Kitty stared at the housekeeper. Receive company? In this dress? She could not possibly—

"Mr. and Mrs. Gardiner just arrived as well. What do you wish me to tell them, Miss?"

Aunt Gardiner? Kitty's eyes prickled. "Would it be all right to show all of them in?"

"The Bingleys and the Gardiners, Miss?"

Bingleys? "Yes, please. Let the kitchen know to prepare for more guests."

The housekeeper nodded. "Mrs. Darcy preferred a particular sandwich—"

"Yes, those would be lovely." She might not be as elegant as Miss Darcy, but Mama had taught her how to properly receive callers.

"Very good, Miss." The housekeeper disappeared.

Kitty pulled several chairs closer to the settee. Uncle Gardiner's hearing had been getting weak, and he liked to sit closer now. She added a small pillow to one chair. Aunt Gardiner usually used one to support her back since her last lying in.

Footsteps approached. Her heart fluttered in time.

"The Gardiners and the Bingleys, Miss." The housekeeper curtsied and left.

They all stared a moment. Kitty giggled. Louisa and Aunt Gardiner joined in. She rushed to kiss their cheeks.

"I cannot tell you how glad I am to see all of you."

"And we you." Uncle Gardiner sat in the chair closest to the settee.

"We did not wish to intrude upon all the diversions of London, but we simply could not miss the opportunity to see you." Aunt Gardiner fluffed the small pillow and settled it behind her. "Miss Bingley, we had no idea of you being in town or we would certainly have called upon you."

"I only just returned from visiting Mr. Hurst's sisters in Lyme. They planned to journey to Shropshire for Twelfth night, but I did not want to leave Charles alone for the holidays."

"Which you would not have done as I—now we—are going to Pemberley to spend Twelfth Night with Darcy."

"The Darcys now," Louisa said.

"Yes, yes of course." Mr. Bingley leaned back a bit and crossed his ankles.

"It is sometimes difficult to think of my sisters as married." Kitty held her breath. What had she just said?

"All of them?" Louisa asked. "Miss Lydia as well? I had not heard." "Yes," Aunt Gardiner said. "It was quite a simple affair, a few months ago. She married a militia officer. They are stationed in the north now."

Dear Aunt Gardiner!

"I imagine she was disappointed with a simple celebration after the grand double wedding." Louisa said.

Oh, when would the tea tray come?

"I believe Lydia managed to have her own way well enough." Aunt Gardiner raised an eyebrow to her husband.

Uncle Gardiner shifted in his seat and braced his elbow on the chair's arm. "So, Bingley, are you still seeking to purchase an estate?"

Mr. Bingley sat a little straighter and glanced at Kitty. "Indeed, I am. Darcy knows of a small place not far from the silk mills in Derby that he thinks might suit me well enough."

"And the proximity to the mills does not hurt, eh?"

Mr. Bingley chuckled. "No, it does not. I hear they are looking for investors. It seems to me the world is turning to industry—"

"Precisely what I told my brother Bennet—"

Aunt Gardiner laid her hand on her husband's. "You gentlemen may call upon each other later to discuss business prospects."

Uncle Gardiner laced his fingers with hers and smiled.

The housekeeper entered with a large tea tray and placed it on the table near the settee.

Kitty opened the tea caddy. "Aunt? Uncle?"

"Yes, please."

She might not have mastered the finest points of table manners nor perfected a graceful, deep curtsey, but Kitty knew how to serve the perfect cup of tea and was most pleased to do so.

"Are these the sandwiches we enjoyed at Longbourn?" Mr. Bingley took a bite. "They were a favorite of mine." He spoke through the mouthful.

"Yes, I think Lizzy brought the receipt here—" Kitty peered over Mr. Bingley's head. She rose. "May I present Miss Darcy's companion, Mrs. Hartwell? Would you care for tea?"

Mrs. Hartwell curtsied and approached them. "Thank you, no. I must return to Miss Darcy. I came to tell you she has taken ill and will not be able to join you this afternoon."

"How dreadful." Louisa clasped her hands in her lap.

Clearly she did not worry about mussing her gloves.

"Is it serious?" Aunt Gardiner asked.

"Yes. I fear she will not be able to attend Christmas dinner with the Earl and his family tomorrow. I am sorry, Miss Bennet."

Kitty tried to reply, but only stammered. Mrs. Hartwell was far too strict. How unfair! Lydia deprived her society in Meryton, and now Miss Darcy did the same thing to Catherine in London! She clenched her fists and ducked her face. She would not cry, not in company. She could do that well enough alone in her room tonight.

"Should Kitty stay with us for the duration of Miss Darcy's illness?" Aunt Gardiner glanced at her husband.

"I think that might be wise. I do not expect Miss Darcy will be well enough to travel to Pemberley as planned either."

Kitty swallowed hard. She would not go to see Lizzy? She clutched the arm of the settee and fought to draw a breath. This was not her first disappointment. She would not wither. London was very nice and she loved the Gardiners. Her first hopes had been to visit with them—

"Kitty?" Aunt Gardiner asked.

"Oh!" Kitty jumped.

"I believe we can help." Mr. Bingley smiled broadly. "We still intend to go to Derbyshire. Miss Bennet, you would be most welcome to join us."

"Oh, yes!" Louisa clasped her hands before her. "I would enjoy your company very much. I have been trying to arrange for my wedding clothes and could quite use your help."

Three days with her dearest friend, her handsome brother and a trip to Derbyshire? Kitty's hands trembled. "Uncle, may I? Do you think Papa would approve?"

"Miss Bingley is your particular friend and the Darcys desired Mr. Bingley to accompany you and Miss Darcy…" He stroked his chin. "Yes, I do think he would approve. It is a capital solution."

"Oh, thank you!" Kitty bounced in her seat but quickly subdued the impulse.

"You both must join us for Christmas dinner tomorrow, unless of course you have other arrangements. Though we might not be an earl's family, I dare say we can be a merry party." Aunt Gardiner winked.

Mr. Bingley cocked his head at Louisa. "We have no fixed engagements. Christmas dinner ought to be celebrated with a large group of friends and family. There is something melancholy about a small table for that meal."

"I agree. Longbourn would have been so dull this year, with only Aunt and Uncle Philips. I doubt Mama would even come downstairs to join us."

"Is your mother unwell?" Louisa asked.

"She is of a delicate constitution," Aunt Gardiner said. "After four weddings in the span of a year, I fear the strain has taken its toll on her."

"But we do have good hope for her recovery. Your father even talked about taking her to Bath." Uncle Gardiner rubbed his hands together.

"A trip? Papa? He hates to travel."

"Remarkable, is it not? He asked my opinion when he was here. My sister always wanted to visit Bath. It seems the idea has already begun to improve her spirits."

"That is cause to celebrate," Mr. Bingley said.

"Shall I have a maid pack your things?" Mrs. Hartwell asked. "I will send them around when they are ready."

"Excellent." Aunt Gardiner nodded. "It is probably time for us to return home. Will you ride with us or come along later with your trunks?"

"I would prefer to go with you, if I may. I will just get my workbag to take along."

"Of course my dear. Where would you be without a needle in your hand?"

"I will make the arrangements." Mrs. Hartwell curtsied and left.

Mr. Bingley chuckled. "We should be on our way as well. I suppose our cook and maid will consider it quite a gift to prepare only for themselves."

Louisa touched her brother's arm. "Goodness, I hope it will not inconvenience your—"

"Not at all, Miss Bingley. We always seem to entertain unexpected guests for Christmas dinner, and our cook simply expects that now," Aunt Gardiner said.

"May I walk you to the door?" Kitty asked. It was probably poor manners, not that it mattered. Spending a few extra moments with her friends was more important than acting like *Catherine*.

"I would be honored." Mr. Bingley offered one arm to Louisa and the other to Kitty and strolled toward the foyer.

"Oh, look!" Louisa pointed overhead. "A kissing bough!"

Kitty blushed.

"What a fine thing! Miss Bennet?" Mr. Bingley's eyes twinkled, and he kissed her cheek.

His warm lips branded her skin as his breath tickled her ear. She closed her eyes. If only she could tie up this moment in a fancy silk ribbon to keep in her box of treasures. Why was it over so quickly?

He disengaged his arm from Louisa and plucked a berry. She took it from him and tucked it in his pocket with a wink.

Kitty's face burned, and she struggled most unsuccessfully to hide her smile. If he thought she intentionally moved to the kissing bough, he did not seem displeased, nor did Aunt and Uncle Gardiner. Perhaps she was not so improper after all.

They lingered several moments at the carriage. It was hard to see them go, almost as difficult as when they left after Lizzy and Jane's wedding. But she would see them soon, unlike Miss Darcy who would likely be devoid of company for quite some time.

On the way to her rooms, raised voices filtered into the corridor. Miss Darcy and Mrs. Hartwell were quarreling.

Listening in was most improper, but how else did a fourth sister get her information? She stole down the hall and stood near Miss Darcy's door.

"It is not fair! You deprived me of our callers today. Now you are sending away my only company in months, and you will not let me go visit my brother. I am a prisoner!"

Had Lizzy intended for Mrs. Hartwell to be so harsh? It did not seem possible.

"Do you believe your behavior warrants any of the privileges you name? Have you forgotten everything your aunt taught you? You were doing so well before she came. I thought you were ready to rejoin your family's company. I am sorely disappointed in you."

Kitty pressed her first to her mouth. This was why people should not eavesdrop. One ran the unpleasant risk of hearing awful things said about oneself.

"I do not blame Miss Bennet's influence—"

"But her manners—"

"May be somewhat unpolished, but she possess qualities far more important—those which your brother hoped you would acquire under Lady Matlock."

"I know—I know. Must you continually remind me?" Miss Darcy sniffed. "She is thoughtful and kind, industrious and good, and very pretty beyond all that. I am not sure I like having a sister to be compared against. Have you any idea how tiresome it is to be told how you do not measure up to someone else, and if you do not do better, no one will want you?"

"Yes, I do." Kitty whispered. How strange to hear her own sentiments spoken by another. Even stranger—standing in Lizzy's and Jane's shoes brought her little joy. How could something so complimentary leave her so heavy and sad?

"And do not forget, you have disappointed Miss Bennet as well. Imagine how much she anticipated the Matlock's dinner."

"She can still go without me."

"Perhaps in the strictest sense, you are correct. I expect though, she will not attend. How could she dare go into so great a house, knowing she is not equal to their company? You should have had greater consideration for your friend. Can you see now why I say you are not fit for company?"

Apparently neither was Kitty, but at least she could escape Mrs. Hartwell. Kitty returned to her chamber and retrieved her work bag. Perhaps it would have been better had she never left Longbourn.

The Gardiner's carriage was well-worn, not nearly as comfortable as Miss Darcy's, but the company was easy and warm. Their second-rate town home welcomed her with firelight in the windows and excited voices behind the door.

Young Gardiners mobbed her, talking over each other, vying for her attention. How much they had all grown. Thomas had been an infant in arms the last time she had seen him.

Tears prickled her eyes. This is what had been missing from Longbourn these cold, lonely months. How dearly she loved company and the chaos of a house full of family. The children pulled her hands and begged her to join them hanging greenery throughout the house.

She drew a deep breath filled with evergreen, baking shortbread and kin. Christmastide at last, exactly as she had longed for.

Uncle peeked in. "Your trunks arrived from Darcy House. I sent them to your room."

"Let me help you settle your things." Aunt helped Kitty to her feet. "I do not imagine you wish to unpack everything since you will be leaving soon."

Aunt wore a peculiar expression. Unpacking was utterly irrelevant. She wanted to talk and would not be denied. Just as well, after the months of Mama's lethargy, it would be pleasant to finally talk to someone who cared.

Aunt sat on the bed as Kitty knelt beside the largest trunk. A pretty hatbox perched atop the trunk. Her eyes burned. Best not open it now. She moved it aside and lifted the trunk's lid.

"I will not need it now, but I must show you the gown my sisters had made for me." She shook out the folds and held it up.

"For dinner at the Earl's house?"

"Yes."

"It is lovely. The color suits you well. Are you very disappointed you will not be able to attend?"

Kitty bit her lip and folded the gown into the trunk. "My feelings are so mixed, I hardly know."

Aunt patted the counterpane and slid over. "Tell me about them, dear, all of them."

"I am happy to be with here with you in Cheapside. It is ever so nice to be in a home with smiles and laughter and people again."

"I imagine Longbourn very lonely for you since your sisters left."

"Terribly lonely. I thought perhaps, Mama would...would have time for me since I was the only one left. But..." She ran her tongue along the roof of her mouth. "...her nerves—the apothecary called it the vapors and gave her a draught that calms her so much she does little more than sleep."

"Your father is no more attentive to you?"

"No, he is so concerned for Mama that I only get in the way."

"I am so sorry."

Kitty gasped and shoved her fist to her mouth. She breathed hard until she found the control she sought. "Only Charlotte Lucas still speaks to me. The whole of Meryton turned on me because of *her*." She covered her face with her hands and panted hard. Only little girls and Kittys cried—not Catherines. "The one time in my life with no other Bennet sister to command attention, and no one will see me because of Lydia. She is not even here to bear the effects herself."

Aunt slid her arm over Kitty's shoulders. "This trip must have meant a great deal to you."

Kitty pressed into her and nodded. "I did look forward to that dinner. It seemed things were finally changing."

"And now?"

"It is just as well I am not going."

Aunt pulled her closer. "What happened?"

Kitty sniffled. "After staying with Miss Darcy, it became clear my manners...well, everything about me is not up to her level of society."

"How did you come by that notion?"

"Mrs. Hartwell."

"I cannot imagine her saying such a thing—"

"Mrs. Hartwell is so very strict. I am not sorry to have left her company, but I should thank her for delivering me from making a fool of myself."

"You have lovely manners and are charming company."

"Even if that is true, none of that mattered in Meryton, and apparently it matters little in London either." She pushed to her feet and paced between the bed and trunks. "I am so angry I can hardly speak. I know it is wrong, but I hate Lydia. This is all her fault. What is worse, Miss Darcy is little different. She is as stupid and foolish as Lydia and will likely try to elope as soon as the opportunity presents." Kitty bit her knuckle. Had she just said that? How could she ever be allowed in society when she could not control her own tongue?

"She already did."

"What did you say?" Kitty's brow furrowed into a painful knot, the kind her threads tangled into when she was careless whilst mending.

"Before Mr. Darcy went to Meryton, his sister nearly went off with a most unsuitable young man who is now in the Navy. She was sent to her aunt's for improvement."

"I do not think she has improved very much."

"Neither did Lizzy, which is why I recommended Mrs. Hartwell. We both felt Miss Darcy needed someone with a firmer hand."

"She is taking a very firm hand indeed. I am glad she is not my companion. I am surprised you found her an acceptable candidate."

"I am sorry you do not like her."

Kitty shrugged. "I just do not understand why Lydia—a married woman—should go and make merry among the soldiers, free from all the trouble she left behind for me."

"Has Lydia written you recently?"

"No," Kitty tossed her head and snorted. "She has not the time with balls and parties every night."

"Is that what she told you?"

"Yes, in the only letter she wrote me."

"Wait here a moment." Aunt left and returned moments later, several letters in hand. "I do not make a habit of sharing my correspondence, but I think you might be interested in what she writes."

"I do not desire to hear of her gowns and popularity."

"Read her letters. You may give them back to me tomorrow or the next day." She pressed the small pile at Kitty and left.

Kitty tossed them aside. Why would she ever want to read anything from Lydia ever again? Heartless, foolish girl.

She turned to her trunks and unpacked enough for a short stay. The letters watched her from the bed, taunting and teasing in Lydia's best sing-song voice. Something fluttered in her stomach like wet laundry set out to dry.

Catherine should obey the wishes of her aunt. No, not yet, Kitty had things to do.

Far too soon, her tasks were accomplished. She sat on the bed and stared at the pile of correspondence.

Lydia's hand was not pretty. Letter writing was not the kind of accomplishment she could be bothered to perfect. Kitty picked up the oldest one and unfolded it. The note was short, not cross written by many lines the way Lizzy's would have been.

> *Dear Aunt Gardiner,*
>
> *Kitty wrote to say what a dither Mama is in, so I dare not write to ask her. Naturally I thought of you.*
>
> *We are in a small situation here in Newcastle, smaller than I expected. But, as there are few houses to let, we try to be merry in our few rooms. Though the house is small, there is a great deal more work to be done than I expected and I have only one maid-of-all-work to do it. I work so very hard all day. I barely have strength to pick up my pen.*
>
> *I must beg you to send me some receipts. I need to know how to make a stomach tincture and how to prepare lye for soap. No doubt you know these things, so please, do send them soon. Oh, and can you include receipts for any kind of food that can be cheaply made as well?*
>
> *If you might have a pound or two to spare, that would be lovely, too.*
>
> *LH*

The gall of her, asking Aunt for money! Lydia was a married woman with a husband to provide such things for her. But she lived in a small house with only one maid. Kitty worried her bottom lip in her teeth.

Lydia must have changed pens for the second letter bore few of her characteristic loops and flourishes. The script was small and tight and it was written on a very small scrap of foolscap.

> *We moved again for the rent on the house was too high. I had to dismiss the maid. We live in a small cottage now that we share with Lt. Carter and Olivia Bond. I thought it would be jolly fun to live with them as Olivia and I were such chums in Meryton. She married not long before I—or did you already know that? In any case, I was wrong.*
>
> *She is very angry at me for encouraging her to elope. She misses Meryton and the ease of her family's situation and blames me.*
>
> *Lt. Carter says he is tired of listening to it all so he and Harper stay away from the cottage for long stretches. I am very lonely. I think Olivia and Lt. Carter will move soon. Perhaps we will find a more agreeable housemate. Could you send a receipt for the poppy tea Hill makes for Mama's nerves? If you have a few shillings to spare, that would be very welcome, too.*
>
> *LH*

Serves her right! Kitty slapped the letter. Lydia could not enjoy having Olivia's sharp tongue turned on her. Perhaps Lydia was hearing the same things from Olivia that Margery had said to her.

To be subject to it in her own home, though? Kitty's shoulders sagged. At least she had respite in the walls of Longbourn. Lydia had not even that. Bile burned her tongue. How dire were Lydia's circumstances? Did Papa know?

Trembling hands opened the third letter.

> *This has been a difficult month for us. Harper was injured whilst drilling the men. The surgeon dug the musket-ball from his shoulder, but the wound is not healing well. I remember a poultice Mama learned from Lady Lucas. I should like to use it for him, so please, if you know it, write very soon.*
>
> *Since you have so many children of your own, will you tell me what the signs are when one is increasing? I cast up my accounts several times a day. Harper thinks I have not the stomach for the sick bed. But I am not certain that is the problem. I do hope my belly is not full. Our new cottage mates will not be apt to look well upon an infant. I do not know how I can pay a midwife or wet nurse. I shall watch for your letter. If you have any shillings to spare—*

Kitty set the letter aside and hugged her knees to her chest. How lonely Lydia must be. Was her cottage as dark and drafty as the Blacks'? Did she go hungry? Surely she did. Was she with child? Kitty rocked back and forth. Her spine scraped against the headboard.

Oh, Lydia! As bad as Meryton had been, it was nothing to what Lydia endured. Poor foolish girl—all her dreams dashed, and now her husband ill, and she might be increasing? Were Lizzy and Mary and Jane aware? Surely they would want to help. Perhaps Aunt would allow her to bring these letters for them to read as well.

Truly, Lydia was hoist with her own petard, but still, to live in a hovel like the Blacks! She shuddered. What a price to pay for her foolishness!

How strange to feel sorry for her now. To be sure, the anger was not entirely gone, but the dull stabbing pain in her belly had eased. Was it forgiveness? She did not know.

That night, at sunset, Uncle lit the tall, stout Yule Candle. He placed it in the middle of the Yule-heap of cakes and loaves of breads to be kept fresh by the Yule Candle light. The children placed their favorite toys and trinkets in the circle of its glow. Would they really last longer because of the candle's light? Even if they did not, she would not tell her cousins otherwise.

"It is so good you are here with us!" Silas bounced in his seat. "Last year our housekeeper sat with us for dinner to make us an even number at the table."

"She was ever so cross at being kept from her work." Alice, the eldest, folded her napkin in her lap.

"Well, I am pleased to join you." Kitty helped Silas tuck his napkin into his collar. His own efforts would hardly protect his shirt.

"Remember, we must all leave the table together, else there will be bad luck." Alice glared at Margaret who slumped in her seat and pouted.

Uncle cleared his throat. "Before we consider leaving the table or even enjoying our meal, let us consider what acts of charity we might perform between Christmas and Twelfth night. There are so many less fortunate than we. It is the season of charity."

Kitty had money left from Mr. Darcy's gift. What was a new bit of finery when her sister was cold and hungry? She would write the letter tonight.

Chapter 7

THE NEXT MORNING, KITTY helped Aunt ready the children for church. There would be no more merry times like these for her at Longbourn. How could she return to that dismal place? Would Pemberley be as welcoming as this?

Four children were challenging to manage. Aunt would surely appreciate help. Perhaps she should ask for permission to stay here with the Gardiners.

The church was so much larger than Meryton's little stone chapel, but the same people filled it: ragged old women who smelled like the mumpers; young ladies with very large hats; dandies who glared at restless little boys just breeched; doting mob-capped mothers who ignored them.

The vicar shuffled papers and adjusted his glasses. "And so, we may understand the underlying message of Christmastide is one of reconciliation; that man might be reconciled to God. In the same way, during this season, let us seek to make reconciliations one with another."

Aunt looked over the heads of her children and caught Kitty's gaze. Kitty pressed her lips together and nodded. It was time to be reconciled to her sister. Lydia was making the best of her situation, and it was surely worse than Kitty's. If Lydia could do it, then so could Catherine.

Her cousins chattered and skipped all the way home.

"Will there be a Christmas pudding, mama?" Silas tugged his mother's hand.

"Do you not remember stirring them up four Sundays ago?"

"Oh yes, I put the charms in. Oh! Oh!" He clapped. "Will it be on fire when it is brought in?"

"You must wait and see, dear."

Silas ran ahead, shouting to Margaret and Thomas of flaming puddings.

"How many will we be at dinner tonight?" Alice asked.

"The six of us, of course, and Kitty makes seven. Mr. and Miss Bingley—"

"Oh! Mr. Bingley is so handsome." Alice batted her eyes. "Will he wear the purple coat he wore at Lizzy and Jane's wedding?"

"I do not know what he will wear. But I do know he is far too old to be interested in so young a girl. Need I be concerned that you will be able to behave properly?"

Alice's shoulders sagged. "I will make you proud, Mama."

"I am sure you will." Aunt patted her back. "The Richards will be attending as well."

"They are both coming?" Alice bobbed up on her toes.

"Yes, a note came from them last night." Aunt turned to Kitty. "Mr. Richards is your uncle's clerk at the warehouse. He and his sister are alone this year. Both their parents recently passed—"

"And Papa cannot stand the thought of anyone suffering a small Christmas feast." Alice giggled.

"He is a kind and generous man." Kitty smiled. "Mama is a great lover of company. We usually host a large Christmas feast, too."

"I believe it a Gardiner family tradition, but sometimes it can be a bit excessive."

"Last year four and twenty came to dinner, and we had no place for them all." Alice giggled.

"Happily everyone was quite good natured with our makeshift arrangements. Though I think your friend Miss Darcy would have been shocked." Aunt winked. "Alice, do be a good girl and run ahead with Silas. See he does not wander off."

Alice dashed off.

Aunt caught Kitty's arm and slowed her until the children were out of earshot. "How are you feeling today?"

"Different, lighter, and determined to enjoy what I have, which is more than I thought I had."

Kitty smoothed her dress and patted her hair one last time. Their guests would arrive soon. It would have been nice to dine at an earl's house, but at least here, she would be surrounded with people who were not examining her to find fault. Uncle and Aunt entertained in true Gardiner fashion. It would be a merry evening.

Her beautiful evening gown remained folded in her trunk, her hat in its box. Instead, she wore a pretty dinner dress pieced from an old dress of Jane's and one of Lizzy's. Although the muslin, marcella and jaconet she used were not new, she had carefully cut around the few stains and tears. With new ribbons, some lace, and the most fashionable patterns, the dress might well have been made for Catherine by a Bond Street modiste. Hopefully, Mr. Bingley would approve.

She paced the room, wringing her hands. He had been so kind to invite her to travel with them, even without Miss Darcy, but he was thoughtful and kind to everyone. It did not necessarily hold that he felt anything more than friendship for her. More likely it was friendship for Mr. Darcy. Still, back in Hertfordshire, he seemed to prefer her company. At least he did once he had stopped staring at Jane.

She turned on her heel and pumped her fists. Oh, this whole business was most vexing indeed! Perhaps she might draw Louisa away for a few minutes and ask her thoughts on the matter.

The clock chimed a quarter to the hour. Enough nervous fluttering, she must get below stairs.

All the Gardiners gathered in the parlor. The children were dressed and polished, pretty as china dolls. Silas tugged at his lacy collar and kicked his feet along the front of the settee whilst little Thomas squirmed beside him, eyeing Silas' breeches. Poor little boy wanted a skeleton suit of his own so badly. Alice whispered something to her younger sister, Margaret, and they tittered. Perhaps breeches would be presented to Thomas for Twelfth Night. She must ask Aunt if it were so and offer to add a bit of embroidery or other fancy work to the suit.

"Oh, Kitty, you look beautiful." Margaret rushed to Kitty's side. Pudgy little fingers spread her skirt and traced the embroidered scrolls.

"Your dress is so elegant." Alice peered over Margaret's shoulder.

"Did you embroider it yourself?" Aunt asked.

"I did. I remade it from my sisters' old gowns. I saw two different patterns and could not choose between, so I combined them into this." She twirled to show the back of the dress.

"Oh, oh! You must show me how to do the lacework on the sleeves!" Alice ducked behind Kitty and ran her fingertips along the delicate work. "You are so very clever."

"I will be happy to teach you. It is not so hard—"

The housekeeper appeared. "Mr. and Miss Richards." They stepped in.

He was a young man in a suit neither made nor tailored for him. It hung too loosely on his slight frame. Not so much as to be shabby, but enough to give him the air of a younger brother not quite fitting into his brother's old clothes. Around his arm he wore a black band. The suit must have been his father's. That would also account for the tiny sad lines around his eyes that persisted despite his smile.

His sister was clearly cut of a different cloth. Despite her black shawl and black trimmed bonnet, her smile held no traces of grief. The children rushed to greet her, and she crouched to meet them eye to eye. Little Thomas wrapped his chubby hand in hers and was rewarded with a kiss on the cheek.

"Come in, come in." Uncle went to meet them. "Kitty, may I present Mr. and Miss Richards."

Kitty curtsied.

"Do sit down." Aunt fluffed a pillow on the settee.

Kitty sat beside Aunt. "I understand you are a clerk for my uncle, sir."

"Yes, I have worked for him these three years now."

"And I have been pleased for every one of them." Uncle grinned.

"Where are you from, Miss Bennet?" Miss Richards asked, settling Thomas in her lap.

"My family lives in Hertfordshire, near Meryton."

"Meryton! One of my favorite towns. I love to visit, when we are able to get away from London for a bit."

"Our Aunt Goulding, my mother's sister, lives in Meryton," Mr. Richards said.

Kitty sucked in a short breath before she could stop herself. No, it was not possible. Of all people, did it have to be Mrs. Goulding?

Silas ran to the window. "Look, another carriage!"

"Our other guests must be here." Uncle rose.

"Only one carriage worth, sir?" Mr. Richards chuckled. "I expected you to exceed the two dozen of last year with fifty at least."

"If I did, you might find me on your doorstep for Boxing Day. My dear wife is patient, but even saints have their limits!"

"Indeed we do." Aunt rose and shook out her skirt.

They laughed heartily.

The housekeeper appeared again. "The Bingleys."

Mr. Bingley and Louisa entered, he grinning broadly, she a bit more shyly.

"I say, that is precisely the sound I would be greeted with. Do share the joke with me that I might partake as well."

Uncle bowed and made introductions. "We just learned Richards has ties to Meryton."

"Indeed? A lovely little town it is." Mr. Bingley dropped into a chair between Kitty and Mr. Richards. He stretched his long legs and balanced his elbows on his knees. "Do tell me of your connections. Have you spent a great deal of time there?"

"Not as much as we would like in recent years. We spent our childhood summers in the country with Aunt Goulding," Miss Richards said.

"They were memorable ones. So lovely to be away from the confines of the city." Mr. Richards shifted in his seat. "What are your links to Meryton?"

Mr. Bingley glanced at Kitty and smiled the sparkling-eyed smile that sent her heart fluttering. "We met Miss Kit—Bennet several months ago whilst we let a house there. Are you familiar with Netherfield Park?"

"Oh, yes," Miss Richards said. "It was a lovely place as I remember, though I thought the owner, Mr. Bascombe, something dreadful."

Mr. Richards wagged his brows. "We were playing along the banks of a small stream and must have wandered onto his property. The poor man was so cross with us. He scolded until he turned quite red in the face."

"I thought he might suffer an apoplexy in the middle of the meadow." She giggled.

Mr. Bingley gazed at Miss Richards.

Kitty bit her knuckle. Did he find her attractive? She was uncommonly pretty and charming.

"He has not changed considerably. That sounds much like the man with whom I negotiated the lease."

Miss Richard's lips bunched into a tight frown. "Our Aunt mentioned a fire at Netherfield in one of her letters. Someone killed falling out a window? Do tell me that was not during your tenure."

Kitty gulped.

Mr. Bingley tugged his collar.

"Forgive me for interrupting. I believe dinner is ready." Aunt rose.

"We must not keep the food waiting." Mr. Bingley jumped to his feet and offered her aunt his arm.

Kitty bit her lip. He was only being polite, escorting his hostess. Why should that cause her chest to pinch so? Mr. Richards escorted Louisa. Thomas toddled to Miss Richards and dragged her toward the dining room. Silas bowed to Kitty with great solemnity, leaving Uncle to escort his daughters.

By the time they reached the dining room, Thomas was in Miss Richards's arms, chatting softly to her. Her ease with Thomas only added to her beauty. No wonder Mr. Bingley kept looking at her.

Kitty hung back as the party seated themselves. Louisa caught her gaze and nodded toward the chair next to Mr. Bingley. Kitty blushed and took the seat.

Candles glittered among the heaping platters of roast boar's head, cod and a huge roast goose. A tureen of mock turtle soup sat near Aunt, surrounded by stewed cucumbers, roast potatoes and beans ragooed with parsnips.

Uncle carved the meat and served slices. The adults nearest the children assisted them.

"Is this Mama's soup receipt?" Kitty asked.

Aunt winked. "Actually it came from your great grandmother Carlson who passed it to your Grandmother Gardiner, who gave it to your mother, who gave it to me."

"It will pass through yet another generation as I copied it to my own book—for someday." Kitty dropped her gaze.

"I wish my mother kept such a book to share with me." Miss Richards sighed.

"Did something happen to it?" Louisa asked.

"No, I fear she did not read and write herself."

"I do not like to read and write." Silas sat crossed his arms over his chest.

"Hush." Alice elbowed him. "How can you be like Papa if you do not read?"

"You enjoyed the last story I read to you." Miss Richards wagged her finger at him.

Mr. Richards chuckled. "I enjoy the way you allow the children at the table for Christmas dinner. They are delightful. Have you any brothers or sisters, Miss Bennet?"

"Yes, I am the fourth of five sisters."

"Where are they?"

"They...they are with their husbands."

"Your younger sister is married too? I did not think it the way of the gentry," Mr. Richards murmured.

Kitty's face burned. She turned aside.

"My sister, their mother, does not hold to that convention." Uncle said. "My dear, shall I call for the second course?"

"Yes, I believe we are finished." Aunt cast a meaningful look at Kitty who ducked away.

The housekeeper and maid cleared the first course and tablecloth beneath, decorated with drips of sauce and gravy. Platters and bowls and plates, including one heaped with minced pies, appeared on the pristine new cloth.

"Oh, my favorite!" Margaret squealed, pointing to the black butter.

"It is a favorite of mine too, Miss Margaret." Miss Richards smiled and spooned some onto Margaret's plate.

"You are a clerk for Mr. Gardiner?" Mr. Bingley asked. "I never had a head for detail. I leave that to my friend Darcy. I find I prefer making plans and—"

"Dreaming up new ideas." Louisa grinned, eyes twinkling to match his. "Our father was much the same. It made him successful in business."

"I hope to own a business someday," Mr. Richards said.

"Really? What kind of business?" Mr. Bingley dabbed the corner of his mouth.

"He wants to work his way up to be partner to me." Uncle leaned across the table and clapped Mr. Richard's shoulder.

"That is many years off I am sure. I would prefer to begin a bit sooner. Something small perhaps. I wish my sister to stay home with me and help keep shop rather than hire out as a governess out of the reach of my protection."

"My brother is too kind and exceedingly protective."

"One cannot be too protective of a young lady's reputation or person." Mr. Richards folded his arms over his chest.

Kitty held her breath. What decided opinions he professed and so freely too!

"What kind of shop had you in mind?" Mr. Bingley braced his elbows on the table and rubbed his palms together.

Mr. Richards and Uncle launched into an animated discussion of options to which Alice, Margaret and Silas added their share to the conversation.

As they finalized their plans for the first confectionary-toy-bakery-haberdasher's shop in all London, Aunt cried, "Christmas pudding anyone?"

The children clapped and shouted as the housekeeper brought in a spectacular flaming pudding and placed it in the center of the table. Thomas's eyes grew round and he barely breathed, staring into the dancing blue flames.

When the last one flickered away, Uncle set to serving it.

Silas immediately took a large spoonful.

"Do be careful." Aunt pointed to the pudding. "Remember the charms inside."

Silas stopped his spoon midway to his mouth and returned the large morsel to his plate. He split it with a resounding metallic clink. He squealed and held up a penny.

"Look! I will be rich!"

"I want one too!" Thomas cried.

"Eat your pudding and perhaps you will find something." Miss Richards handed him a spoon.

Kitty hesitated. Butterflies fluttered her belly. Last year, a spinster's thimble appeared in her pudding. Mama and Lizzy laughed it away. Dear Mary suggested it stood for her love of needle work, not spinsterhood. Lydia, though, tormented her about it for months, secreting the charm in the most unexpected places. Oh please, let there be no a charm at all this year.

"Oh, look!" Alice cried and held up a tiny shoe.

"Where shall you travel? Perhaps a grand tour?" Mr. Bingley asked.

Louisa dangled a miniature horseshoe over her fingertip. "I do believe I have already felt my good luck."

"Her betrothed is returning from the continent sooner than expected." Mr. Bingley nodded at her.

No thimble, yet. Kitty ate slowly, savoring each rich bite. The more the piece on her plate shrank, the less likely it contained that dreaded—

"Oh, ow!" Mr. Richards pressed his cheek and pulled a petite thimble from his mouth.

Margaret laughed and pointed. "He should not have that. A man cannot be a spinster."

Mr. Richards set the charm on the edge of his plate. "Too true, Miss Margaret. Perhaps you would like it."

"Oh, no! Not me! I shall have a handsome husband one day."

"Give it to Kitty!" Silas shouted.

Kitty choked on a bit of her pudding, coughing so hard tears stung her eyes.

"Silas!" Aunt glared at him. "If you cannot be pleasant company at my table, you may take yourself to the nursery."

"I am sorry," he mumbled.

Kitty gulped a bit of wine and forced a smile. She took her last bit of pudding. Something hard met her tongue, and she gasped at the odd metallic tang. She spat the small object into her hand and cleaned it with her napkin.

"A ring!" cried Thomas.

"Kitty found the ring." Margaret rose up on her knees to get a better view.

"Lucky!" Alice pouted.

"But who will she marry?" Thomas asked, peering up at Miss Richards.

Louisa smiled at her brother. Was that a wink, too?

"A delightful pudding, my dear. Even better than last year's." Uncle pushed back from the table and patted his belly. "We should say our grace now."

Everyone bowed their heads as he offered a heartfelt prayer of thanksgiving.

"You say the same thing every year, Papa," Alice said.

"Every year it is true. I suppose you ladies would like to adjourn and send the children off to bed." Uncle's lips twitched up at the corners, and his eyes crinkled at the edges.

"No!"

"No, please father."

"Games, please. We want games!" Silas pounded the table with his palms.

"Carols, let us sing carols!" Margaret stood on her chair. Aunt snatched her off and settled Margaret into her lap.

Uncle stroked his chin. "Ah well, since it is Christmas, I suppose, in the spirit of good will and merriment, we might all go to the drawing room together."

The children cheered, and the party adjourned to the parlor. In the family's absence, the servants had rearranged the room and left the makings of any number of games.

"May we sing first, Mama?" Alice clasped her hands before her.

"Yes, we may." She led them to the old harpsichord.

Oh, Aunt would play tonight! "What an excellent suggestion," Kitty whispered in Alice's ear.

Mama said the harpsichord came from Grandmother Gardiner's parlor, but she had little use for such an old fashioned, muddy sounding instrument. She preferred the pianoforte inherited with Longbourn.

Aunt sat at the bench, and Alice ran to the shelf for music. Everyone arranged themselves around the long instrument. Alice adjusted several sheets of music and slid beside her mother. They played a chord several times until Alice mastered the fingering. Aunt nodded and sang.

Whilst Shepherds watched their flocks by night,

Everyone joined in.

All seated on the ground;
The Angel of the Lord came down,
And glory shone all round.

The children's voices, high and pure, trilled out the melody whilst the men wove in a bass line that gave rich solemnity to the familiar carol.

The funny, plucky tones of the harpsichord fit the carol so much better than the smoother quality of the pianoforte. Kitty stroked the worn finish. It was silly to prefer this old, unfashionable thing, or so Mama said, but did she nonetheless.

"Do play another! It has been far too long since I had the opportunity to enjoy a well-played harpsichord." Mr. Bingley patted the top of the instrument.

Kitty peeked at him and smiled.

"This one, Mama, please." Alice moved a sheet of music to the front and played the opening notes.

Kitty's shoulders slumped. Not this one.

Let all that are to mirth incline'd,
Consider well, and bear in mind,
What our good God for us has done,
In sending his beloved son.
For to redeem our souls from thrall,
Christ is the Savior of us all.

Both Mr. Bingley's and Louisa's voices waned on this verse. Why should they dislike it as much as she?

The final notes ebbed away.

Aunt suggested a hand of cards. Louisa and the Richards joined her at the card table.

"What say you," Mr. Bingley crouched beside Silas, "we have a game of bullet pudding?"

Silas grabbed his hands and dragged him to a small table already draped with a cloth, a shining pewter bowl filled with flour in the center.

"Will you play with us?" Margaret tugged Kitty's skirt.

"I...I..." This was certainly not a game for Catherine, not when it might end with her sputtering and snorting and covered with flour.

"Help me play. Mama says I am not big enough to use a knife." Margaret blinked at her, big eyes pleading.

"I will help you play." Kitty sat at the table and balanced Margaret in her lap.

Mr. Bingley scooped the flour into a towering pile on the tablecloth and balanced a bullet at the peak. He handed a large knife to Silas. "You cut it first."

Silas studied the pile from one side then the other. Standing on tiptoes, he drew the knife through the flour and sliced off a generous portion. The bullet remained balanced at the top. He passed the knife to Kitty.

"Hold it with me." Kitty wrapped Margaret's fingers around the handle and her own over her cousin's. "Just a small bit now."

"Do you suppose Mr. Darcy plays bullet pudding with Lizzy and Mr. Bradley now?" Kitty giggled and gave Mr. Bingley the knife.

"I doubt that. Though she has transformed him enough to play games, I cannot imagine the Master of Pemberley at risk of putting his face in a pile of flour—" He sliced through the flour and passed the knife to Silas.

He cut away another large slice, and the bullet toppled into the flour.

"—like my young friend here will have to."

"Awww—" Silas dropped the knife on the table and dove, face first, into the flour, rooting about until he rose with the bullet in his teeth.

Kitty snickered and handed him a towel. "At least you learnt not to laugh whilst you are searching. Flour up your nose is not a pleasant thing."

"No indeed." Mr. Bingley took the towel from Silas and polished the boy's cheeks. "But it is most amusing to watch."

He would wish to see her covered in flour?

Mr. Bingley brushed his palms on the table. "I am sorry Miss Darcy is not able to enjoy our merriment though. She is missing a great deal of fun."

Kitty picked up the towel and wiped a dab of flour from his temple. "I hardly imagine this is what they would be doing at an Earl's house after Christmas dinner." What would they be doing? Who might she have met there? If only...

"I met the Earl and his family, with Darcy, of course."

"You keep very grand company."

Mr. Bingley shrugged. "They are not a bad sort of folk, but I expect you are quite right. They are quite fixed on what is proper, though I suppose they find amusement in their own way. I found it a bit stifling and expect it would be difficult for a girl like Miss Darcy to flourish under all that politeness."

"Truly?" Kitty stared. "Forgive my surprise, but your sister, Miss Caroline is so particular—"

He shuddered. "Please do not remind me! Though she may be fond of high society. I do not consider her in possession of fine manners." The light faded from his eyes, and his voice dropped very low. "I hope you will forgive me and Louisa for Caroline's transgressions. I cannot tell you how much I have regretted the...the deplorable things she said and did."

Kitty cocked her head and squinted at him. What a curious thing to be concerned about now. "It is forgotten—truly she is no worse than many who inhabit Meryton. Lizzy and Mr. Darcy overcame the damage she caused well enough—I see no lasting harm."

"I was thinking about the harsh things she said to you. I recall a particular afternoon when you and Louisa discussed wedding clothes—"

"Oh, yes." Kitty winced. No suggestion she made escaped Miss Caroline's scathing opinions.

"You need not pretend otherwise. She treated you horribly. I never properly apologized. Please allow me—"

"I would not judge you by your sister any more than…than I should wish to be judged by…" She bit her lip and looked away.

"You are most kind."

She peeked at him. When had the sparkle left his eyes? Was it because of Miss Caroline…or Lydia?

"A game of cards?" Mr. Richards stood up at the card table and beckoned them, a slightly worn deck of cards in his hand.

"I think my nieces and nephews—"

"I believe Mr. Gardiner has them quite occupied." Mr. Richards pointed with his chin.

In the far corner, the children sat at their father's feet, entranced. He held tiny figures in his hands. More waited on the table beside him. They paraded across the blanket on his lap, playing out the tale he told.

"He is the best storyteller I know." Kitty clasped her hands under her chin. "He used to do that for my sisters and me."

"Do you want to join them?" Mr. Bingley asked.

She hesitated. Lydia thought it childish and surely Miss Darcy would as well. Would he approve?

Mr. Bingley offered his arm. "We will join cards later."

Mr. Richards nodded and sat down. Mr. Bingley escorted Kitty to her uncle. They sat on the floor with the children. Soon Thomas found his way into her lap and Margaret into his. By the end of Uncle's tale, the two littlest ones slept in their laps, and the elder two yawned.

"Shall we carry them upstairs?" Mr. Bingley whispered.

"Please." Uncle rose and took Alice and Silas by the hands.

Kitty shifted Thomas to her shoulder and followed Uncle upstairs. She led Mr. Bingley to the nursery and pointed to Margaret's little bed near the window. Thomas did not stir as she laid him in his bed, removed his shoes and tucked a blanket over him. Dear little boy—she kissed his forehead and turned to leave.

"Oh!" Mr. Bingley stood so close she nearly ran into him.

He scooted back several steps and mouthed— Excuse me.

They padded out and eased the door shut.

She pressed her finger to her lips and her ear to the door. Silence. "Thank you. I could not have carried them both."

"They are very dear children." Mr. Bingley licked his lips. "I...I am most glad I encountered you here, in London I mean. Though I suppose we would have met at Pemberley in any case—"

"No, with Miss Darcy's...illness...I do not think...I would not have been able to go at all had we not met earlier." How could she string words together when he stood so near? The smooth scent of sandalwood surrounding him did not help. Was her heart's thrumming loud enough for him to hear?

"But, Darcy did ask me to travel along—" He ran a finger along the inside of his collar.

"True enough."

"Whatever the case, I am glad—"

A door shut, and they jumped.

"Asleep before I tucked the blankets around them." Uncle thumbed his lapels.

Mr. Bingley glanced at her once more and sighed.

What dreadful timing. What had he been about to say?

Uncle brushed past her.

"How many times did you settle us girls to sleep the same way?" Kitty followed him down the corridor.

"Enough to be invited to spend Christmas at Longbourn every year."

Laughter filtered from the parlor.

"Just in time for a new hand!" Mr. Richards called over his shoulder.

He and Louisa pulled several chairs to the card table.

"What shall we play now?" Miss Richards scooted her chair to accommodate the newcomers.

"A hand of speculation perhaps?" Mr. Richards shuffled the cards.

"A capital idea." Mr. Bingley tapped the table. "I have not played in months."

"That is because you always win." Louisa folded her arms.

"Why should I be punished for that? It is not my fault if you do not pay proper attention to your cards."

They all guffawed.

Mr. Richards dealt the cards and turned up the trump.

"I do believe you hold something against me, Mr. Richards." Aunt tucked her cards into a neat fan.

"If he has aught against you, then he must be looking to be sacked, given the hand he dealt me." Uncle touched Kitty's shoulder with his.

"The luck of the cards, my friends, nothing more, nothing less." Mr. Richards tapped the remaining cards on the table.

A little smile played along Louisa's lips. "My cards reveal you harbor a secret tendre' for me—one my betrothed might find objectionable."

Mr. Bingley nearly choked on a raucous laugh.

How Kitty loved that sound. Did Catherines laugh? Etiquette manuals suggested not. She chewed the inside of her cheek.

Laughter had filled Longbourn during her childhood. As Mama's concerns for the business of getting husbands occupied more and more of her energies there seemed to be less and less of that precious sound. Given the choice, Kitty would rather stay here in Cheapside, with warmth and worn carpets, laughter and fewer candles, than in the fine houses of Darcy's neighborhood.

"Miss Bennet?" Mr. Bingley whispered.

She jumped and stared at her cards.

"Wool gathering, my dear?" Uncle raised an eyebrow. "I had no idea we were such dull company."

Kitty turned over a card. "Not dull at all. I was merely considering—"

"Not your next bid, certainly—not if that is your card." Mr. Richards rapped the queen with his long index finger.

"Oh, do not take him to heart." His sister sniffed. "He would tease you to distraction merely to assist you in losing the hand."

"I am not the only one with such a brother?" Louisa tipped her head toward her brother.

"I suppose you would say brothers are most troublesome creatures?" Mr. Bingley elbowed Mr. Richards. "I have not one of my own, so I cannot say directly. However, I may infer sisters are at least every bit as provoking and irksome as any brother. What say you, Richards?"

"No truer words have ever been spoken, sir! Gardiner, you must agree as well, for you have two, three sisters is it?"

Uncle's smile faded just enough for Kitty to notice. Just before she left, Lizzy told her of Aunt Rawls.

"I am not sure I agree." Aunt leaned in. "I have two sisters and three brothers. I assure you my brothers are every bit as vexing as my sisters."

"But to whom do you call when you are in need of assistance? Who do you depend on for help? Your brothers, I am sure." Mr. Richards nodded with an annoying elder brother smile.

Unless of course you have none. Kitty studied the tablecloth's tea stains. That one looked like a sleeping cat.

"While sisters, on the other hand, are most skilled at getting themselves into trouble." Mr. Richards stabbed the tea-stain cat with his fingertips. The tablecloth bunched under his hand.

"I cannot say that is the case with all sisters." Mr. Bingley glanced at Louisa.

"Yes, some are very good and helpful, especially when one has no brothers." Kitty smoothed the tablecloth.

"Indeed, brother." Miss Richards tapped her heel. "Do you suggest I am particularly irksome and disruptive to your life?"

"Best watch yourself now!" Uncle pushed his chair back. "You may find your home a very cold place, indeed, if you persist in that vein."

"You are quite probably correct, and yet, as you further make my point, I shall not be gainsaid. A brother you may grab by the scruff of the neck, dust it up a bit in the back of the house and all things are set to right with a pint at the pub. But with a sister, there are the cold looks, the silence and the tears— oh, the tears and the histrionics! Those are not to be borne."

"So now I am prone to histrionic fits and vapors, am I?" Miss Richards half rose in her chair, eyes twinkling, though her tone did not match. "I suppose you will next say you fear me trying to catch a gentleman in a compromise or running off to Gretna Green with some foolish fellow like those goosecaps in Meryton."

Kitty gasped.

"Had you not heard, Miss Bennet?" Mr. Richards asked. "You see, my sister makes my point exactly. In a recent letter, Aunt Goulding mentioned a rash of elopements and attempted elopements in your own home town. One never worries about a brother eloping."

"One needs not be concerned a properly educated sister will do such a thing, either," Miss Richards said. "I would suppose a family ill-bred enough to produce a daughter prone to eloping would likewise produce a foolhardy and irresponsible son whose only hope of getting a wife would be to—"

"Children!" Aunt slapped the table. "That is quite enough!"

"I quite agree." Mr. Bingley tugged his collar. "I have no desire to discuss difficult siblings." He glanced at Kitty.

The Richardses laughed and tucked chins to chests. "Yes, Mrs. Gardiner."

Uncle chuckled, but Mr. Bingley did not. His and his sister's expressions were so serious. No doubt all the talk of elopements and the stain it brought to a family disturbed them. Did they suspect the truth about Lydia?

The air around her turned thick and stale, insufficient for breath.

"I think I hear Thomas." Kitty dashed out and up to the first landing. The cooler air of the corridor splashed like cold water against her face. She clutched the banister for support as it trickled down her neck and shoulders, cooling the rising heat.

Moonlight mixed with the candlelight, creating a shimmer that glinted off a cut glass vase, filled with fragrant roses. The cool luster soothed Kitty's ragged nerves and the familiar scent of roses, so like Mama's, offered fragile peace.

In Meryton, Mr. Bingley hardly noticed Lydia. He never remarked on her behavior nor even glowered at her. Miss Caroline commanded all his attention and vexation. Could that be the case now? Might his agitation be about his sister, not hers?

Oh, that it might be!

But, what if he wished her away because of Lydia?

She squeezed her temples. If that were so, why would he have come tonight? He was everything polite and amiable, but not the kind to deliberately put himself in the way of unpleasant company.

Still, the look on the Bingleys' faces when Mr. Richards talked of the girls in Meryton eloping— clearly Mr. Bingley would never like her because of it.

But what if he could? Was there any chance of it?

She chewed her knuckle.

"Kitty dear, are the children well?" Aunt called from the foot of the stairs.

"Yes, yes, they are fine." She hurried downstairs, pausing in the parlor doorway. Mr. Bingley was laughing. The dear sound rang a little hollow, and the corners of his eyes did not turn up quite the way they usually did—or perhaps she merely imagined it. He glanced her way, and his smile seemed to brighten. She smoothed her skirt and returned to the party.

Chapter 8

THE SOUNDS OF HUNGRY children rising drove Kitty from her bed. After brief ablutions, she made her way to the morning room, work bag in hand. Her letter to Lydia balanced on top of the chemisette.

Aunt and the children already circled the table. Margaret labored over a picture book whilst Alice carefully sewed something—a doll's dress perhaps? The boys marched tin soldiers across the plains of France—or the corner of the table. She was not sure which.

"Good morning, dear. Did you sleep well?"

"I did, thank you." Kitty sat beside her aunt.

"I am pleased you are well-rested, for you will need it today. Our Boxing Day is quite eventful."

"We are to go to the foundling hospital today." Alice set down her sewing and sat up very straight. "I am finishing my last doll dress for them"

"You uncle supports several charities. The foundling hospital is his particular favorite."

"We always go on Boxing Day and play with the children." Silas added.

"Mama sews all year and brings boxes of clothes for them. She made ever so many shirts and frocks and—"

Margaret ran around the table and peeked over Kitty's shoulder. "And we helped with aprons and caps!"

"I had no idea."

"I am not nearly as talented with a needle as you, but I do like to keep my hands busy." Aunt rose. "First, we must give the servants their boxes, then a quick meal before the foundling hospital. The tradesmen will come in the afternoon. We must be back in time, so let us move along."

The children scurried to put away their things and helped their mother retrieve the servants' boxes that were duly presented to the grateful staff. By the time they finished their breakfast, the loaded coach waited ready for them. Jammed with boxes and bags, the family barely squeezed inside. Uncle and Silas sat in the box outside. Thomas wanted to join them, but Aunt insisted he was not yet old enough, so he sulked in Kitty's lap the entire way.

To her surprise, the foundling hospital was a neat, almost pretty building with a large green behind. A large group of children played there, all neatly, if simply, dressed. The family tumbled out of the carriage and up the short flight of steps. A smartly dressed man, surely the governor, opened the door before uncle could knock.

"Mr. Gardiner, Mrs. Gardiner! How lovely to see you." He had a headmaster's voice and a gentleman's belly. "May I offer you a spot of tea and perhaps biscuits for the children and your guest?"

Aunt smiled. "If you do not mind, our children would very much like to join yours in the yard."

"They will be most welcome."

Aunt nodded, and the children dashed out in search of playmates.

The governor ushered them down a long polished corridor. Happy voices, carried on sunbeams, filtered from the green.

"I think you will be pleased at the progress of our educational programs. I personally implemented many of the suggestions you made."

A nursery maid hurried past, an infant in her arms. She paused and showed Kitty the swaddled baby. A tiny fringe of hair peeked below the cap and dark eyelashes framed wide blue eyes. The edge of the baby's mouth turned up at Kitty.

"New arrival, poor mite. Her mother left her only two days ago. A pretty little thing, ain't she?"

"Yes, she is."

How sad, never to know parents or family. Yet, the babe would be sheltered and fed and prepared to go into service, perhaps work in a shop or her uncle's warehouse, maybe even apprentice with a midwife. Sad though it was, how much better than the alternatives?

The nurse continued on her way. What were her troubles compared to this babe who depended on the charity of others simply to survive?

"Other benefactors of our establishment are in the parlor having tea. May I introduce them?"

"Certainly," Uncle nodded at Aunt. "I am always pleased to meet like-minded individuals."

The governor swung the heavy wooden door open.

"Mr. Gardiner?" Mr. Bingley jumped to his feet.

Louisa set her teacup on the table and rose.

What were they doing here?

"Bingley?"

The governor's bushy eyebrows climbed almost to his hair line. "You are already acquainted?"

"Indeed we are. I had no idea we shared a mutual interest in your fine establishment," Uncle said.

"It never occurred to me to mention." Mr. Bingley bowed from his shoulders, his gaze on Kitty.

"How lovely to see you." Louisa hurried to Kitty and kissed her cheek.

"What a perfect surprise." Kitty sat beside Louisa.

There was no one she wanted to encounter more—or less—at this moment. Had she only been able to gather her wits about her and prepare something sensible to say. Too late now, she could not think over her heart's pounding tattoo.

"The Bingley family has supported us nearly as long as you."

"Indeed?" Uncle chuckled. "I wonder we have not encountered you here before."

"Our sister did not prefer to visit, so I am afraid we did not call as often as Louisa and I would have liked."

"But now we are able to come." Louisa beamed at Kitty. "I am pleased by everything here."

"They do an excellent job with the children." Uncle pulled a chair close.

"Not all such establishments are this clean or well-fitted or the children treated with such kindness." Aunt sat down.

"Thank you, madam." The governor rubbed his hands together. "Once you have finished your tea, would you like a tour or perhaps some of the children to perform—"

"Oh, no! No performances today." Mr. Bingley lifted open hands. "They will come to dread being visited. I certainly do not wish to be known as the bearer of such discomfort."

"You make it sound as though your own school days were arduous," Uncle said.

"Charles preferred the sociability of the school room to the rigor of academics." Louisa inclined her head toward her brother.

"You make it sound as though I were a failure as a student!"

"Not at all. I merely spoke of your enjoyment, not your proficiency."

"I earned excellent marks in school."

"Including the ones from the headmaster's cane for your love of tomfoolery."

Mr. Bingley closed his eyes and shook his head. Deep pink crept up his jaw.

"Teaching masters can be so droll," Kitty said. "I do not recall one with any sense of humor at all." Not that she and her sisters had experience with that many.

"So, I expect you shall be most sympathetic with your own brood of unruly children when they only have a mind for fun and frolic." Aunt turned to Uncle and smirked.

Mr. Bingley fingered his cravat. "I should like to tour the rest of your facility."

The governor rose. "Mr. and Mrs. Gardiner?"

"If you do not mind, may I have a few words with the head of boys and girls? We are aware of a few placements for some of the older children."

"Most excellent. I shall send them in immediately."

"I should like to tour with you if, I may." Kitty rose.

"Go right ahead. I am sure you will finish before we do." Aunt wore her maddening, knowing smile. What prompted it now?

The governor led them down the corridor. He stopped a maid, spoke a few words, and sent her on her way.

He took them through the spacious dining room lined with plain tables and benches, then on to the kitchen. The food was simple, but plentiful enough so none went hungry. Upstairs, large rooms with many beds housed children by age and sex. As it was downstairs, everything was simple, clean and filled with sunshine and fresh air.

"While it is true, not every one of our children has made good, we see few of ours hanged."

"A good thing, I suppose, though I would have never considered it in those terms," Louisa murmured.

"Naturally, madam. You deal with a far better sort of people than do we. We take children from quite dire circumstances. Not all hospitals will. Come—"

He beckoned them to the window and pointed to a tall, dark haired girl with other children gathered close. "Her father hung for thievery and her mother, forgive me, a doxie, died of the pox. She brought the girl here just before she died. The little girl in her arms was left when her mum was sentenced to hang. The boy with the crooked leg, his family died in a fire, and his relatives could not afford to keep him. Nearly all come from criminals and moral degenerates."

"They look very sweet to me," Kitty said.

The governor peered down his nose with a glower that could wither the grass on the green. "Looks are deceiving, Miss. For all that your nieces and nephews may resemble our children, they are very different. They come from better stock. They will grow to be fine and upstanding members of society. Our hopes for these children must be tempered by the firm realization of what kind we are dealing with."

"What are your expectations for *their kind*?" Mr. Bingley asked.

"They can be instructed away from their instincts for wrongdoing to embrace honesty and hard work and so provide for themselves upon leaving here. I admit I was skeptical at the possibility. I am regularly uplifted with reports of our charges well-settled in gainful employ. Let me show you the school room."

Mr. Bingley followed half a pace behind. "You think it nearly impossible, or at least highly unlikely, one might rise above the circumstances of his birth?"

"I only know what I see, sir. Do you not think it is far more likely for a person to sink and reveal the basest elements of their nature than for one to rise? Consider, it only takes one sibling to ruin the reputation of a family. It is widely agreed, the egregious behavior of one proves the underlying character of the family. Does it not? Surely you have seen it as often as I."

Louisa bit her lip and wrung her hands.

"I have heard that said," Mr. Bingley said in a voice more like Mr. Darcy's than his own.

The room wavered. Kitty clutched the wall, tea and biscuits sour in her belly. Even the governor agreed! Lydia left her irretrievably ruined.

Mr. Bingley certainly deserved better than her. He did not even look at her now.

She must give up her foolish fantasy and see him only as an indifferent acquaintance. She swallowed hard and hurried to catch up.

The governor could not resist finding a few of the older children to demonstrate recitations. Though Mr. Bingley squirmed though the entire process, he thanked the boys and girls heartily. He intervened before the governor found any more unwilling victims with the suggestion Kitty had been away from the Gardiners for too long.

He no longer wished to be in her company! At least he was polite enough not to say it outright.

Her eyes stung, and she blinked fiercely. "Yes, perhaps I should return to them."

Mr. Bingley glanced back at her, but she refused to make eye contact.

"As you will." The governor led them back to the parlor.

A boy, gangly and freckled, in pants too short and shirtsleeves too long, stood before Aunt, Uncle and one of the hospital staff.

"Thank you very much, sir!" The boy bowed. "I shall be ready to go first thing in the morning." Clearly he was trying not to grin, but the effort nearly overcame him. He dashed from the room with a peculiar limping gait. His awkward steps shouted with joy.

"Are you certain, Sir?" We have two other boys who—"

"Who demonstrate neither the facility for numbers nor the memory for detail that young man just exhibited," Uncle said.

"Very good, sir. The staff member stood and shook Uncle's hand. "I am relieved to have young Martin placed out. Several others have been unwilling to take him on."

"He will do very well apprenticed in my warehouse."

"And Clara shall make an excellent nursery maid for Mrs. Allen," Aunt said.

"We cannot thank you enough—"

Uncle held up his hand. "Enough, they must still prove their own merit."

"With benefactors like you, they can hardly fail."

"What did you think of your tour?" Aunt asked.

"Capital." Mr. Bingley's voice had not entirely regained its usual easy tone. "Oh, before it entirely slips my mind—"

"Which things are so apt to do." Louisa prodded him with her elbow.

"Indeed!" Mr. Bingley laughed. "We would be most pleased if you might be able to join us tomorrow night for dinner. We will leave for Derbyshire soon, and I do not want to leave without returning your generous invitation."

"How kind of you. I fear we already have obligations for tomorrow, but Kitty will be free to join you. You might consider the duty fulfilled through her." Aunt cocked her head and raised an eyebrow at Kitty.

Kitty started. "Oh, I cannot!" Not after giving him up only minutes ago. This was too cruel. "That is to say—"

"Nonsense—you must!"

Why did he have to look at her with pleading hound-puppy eyes?

Louisa grabbed her hand. "He is right. After all, you are to ride to Pemberley with us soon. You may as well become accustomed to our company before you are trapped three days in a carriage with us."

"Not to mention, it will be a good opportunity to review our travel plans with you and ensure they are to your liking." Mr. Bingley nodded.

"You will relieve your friends from the stress of an unrequited social obligation," Uncle said. "If my sister taught you nothing else, surely she impressed upon you—"

Kitty lifted her hands. "Very well, I shall go."

"Excellent!" Mr. Bingley tugged his lapels straight.

"We do need to be going home." Aunt peeked out the window. "I expect the tradesmen and our warehouse workers will be coming by soon. It would not do to be absent for their visits."

"Of course, we will not keep you." Mr. Bingley bowed. "Until tomorrow then"

"Yes, tomorrow." Kitty curtsied and followed her aunt and uncle out. What had she just agreed to?

As soon as they arrived at the house, Aunt marshaled Alice and Kitty to arrange all the boxes in the housekeeper's office, off the kitchen. They barely finished as the first of a steady stream of callers arrived. They greeted each at the back of the house with a mug of wassail, a plate of bread and cheese, and a box prepared especially for them.

Mama did the same thing at Longbourn each year. Hopefully, she felt strong enough to hand out the boxes today. It always gave her such joy. Perhaps it might help her recover.

So too must Kitty recover from her disappointments. The first step would be accomplished once she could meet Mr. Bingley as an indifferent acquaintance. She would begin tomorrow.

"Do stop pacing." Aunt set aside her sewing. "Here, finish this baby dress. It will calm you."

Kitty took the fabric and flounced into a seat. She stabbed the needle into the dress.

"You are going to dinner. Why do you stalk about like a caged beast? One would think you harbored a *tendre'* for Mr. Bingley with all your fluff and fluster."

"I do not. Miss Bingley—Louisa—is my particular friend. Her brother—"

"—is a fine young man. I give you leave to like him very well."

"I am glad you approve of him, but you do not need to be concerned. I do not like him."

"Then why have you just sewn that sleeve shut?"

"Oh!" Kitty threw the baby dress aside. "I did like him, at one time. I did. But yesterday, when the governor talked of girls like Lydia, you should have seen his face. I cannot change what Lydia has done, so I have given up all interest in Mr. Bingley. I am certain there are other gentlemen who are more forgiving of the failings of one's family—"

"How do you know what he thinks? Have you asked?"

"No—but it is clear—"

"What has he said—"

"Nothing. He is too well mannered to speak it. You can see it in his countenance, in his posture, the way he changes the subject when—"

"So, in truth, you are certain of nothing. It is all conjecture and assumption."

"It is clear!"

"From my vantage point, I see something entirely different. I think—"

"Stop! Please, you sound like Jane." She dashed to the window and clutched the sill. No, now was not the time for tears. She would not arrive at the Bingley's with swollen eyes and red face.

Aunt crossed the room in slow measured steps. "What happened?"

"After...Lydia...I wrote Jane, and I talked to Charlotte. They both insisted Lydia's mischief would come to nothing, that it would not continue to reflect upon me..."

"And?"

"They were wrong."

"But what happened?"

"I did not attend the assembly the month she eloped, or the one after. But I did go the third month."

"And?"

Kitty panted hard. How fitting for her voice to try and escape her now. "No one asked me to dance. People stared at me and made odd faces. I heard them talking behind me, even in front of me, almost as though I were not there. They made little effort to conceal their horrid remarks. I was humiliated."

"I had no idea you suffered so. Why did you not write me?"

Kitty sniffled and shrugged.

"You know can always turn to your uncle and me."

Kitty gulped back a sob. "I cannot face it all again. It is enough to be rejected once."

"But perhaps the Bingleys—"

"Please stop. I have given him up. He deserves a *Catherine*, but I will never be one. I am just Kitty."

"My dear, I believe that is more than you realize ." Aunt kissed her cheek. "The carriage will be around in just a moment."

Kitty wrung her hands and worried the hem of her spencer. Just how long would it take to arrive at the Bingley's house? She drew a deep breath and forced her hands to her lap. It would be a comfortable dinner with pleasant friends, nothing more. They might talk about her visit with the Hursts—oh, and Louisa's wedding clothes, that would be a lovely topic. It could take up a fair part of the evening. If they wanted a game, she would suggest hazard. That was usually pleasant enough to play and would fill the evening nicely. She smoothed her skirts. There, no more reason for concern.

The coach slowed and lurched. The Bingley house stood before her, a second-rate town house like the Gardiners, but larger and more richly appointed. The ironwork alone pointed to greater wealth, if somewhat lesser taste than her aunt and uncle.

No point in hesitation. She squared her shoulders and allowed the coachman to hand her out. The housekeeper, a slight grey-haired woman with a sharp nose and old fashioned mobcap led her to the empty parlor. Miss Caroline probably hired her for the air of aloofness she provided the foyer.

"Miss Bingley will attend you shortly. She said to tell you to make yourself comfortable in the mean." She curtsied and left.

What a cold reception. How odd and very unlike Louisa. Perhaps some household business required her attention. Kitty sat on the settee and folded her hands in her lap.

The clock on the mantle ticked away, oblivious to her discomfort. A quarter of an hour later, Kitty rose. She ambled to the shelves in the corner and examined a five piece garniture collection in blue and white porcelain. Where had it come from? Was it Louisa's or Mr. Bingley's or perhaps their parents'? Was there a story behind it? Nearly everything at Longbourn had one.

She glanced over her shoulder—another quarter of an hour had passed—and continued her circuit of the room. The curtains on the street-facing window were of particularly fine brocade, probably specially imported. The braided trim revealed excellent workmanship, though not what she would have chosen. A fringe would have been much more attractive. Still, someone connected with the family clearly understood textiles.

Tick-tock tick-tock tick-tock. Another quarter hour slipped away.

The shelves on the far side of the window contained many books. Several travelogues of Europe lay open. Richly illustrated, they told of places she secretly longed to visit. Mr. Bingley was the only one she ever told of those dreams. She chewed her knuckle.

The clock chimed. A whole hour alone! Surely she might be justified in taking insult now. She strode to the door and peeked out. Of course, the housekeeper was nowhere to be seen. Whom else could she ask to have the carriage brought around? There had to be someone.

She stepped into the hall. What was that noise coming from upstairs? She edged toward the stairs. A woman was crying, sobbing hysterically. Kitty pressed her fist to her mouth. Louisa!

Her feet set into motion before she had a clear thought of where she was going. The wracking sobs led her upstairs, down the right-hand hall and to a room at the end. The door stood partway open, letting out a sliver of light into the otherwise dim corridor.

Kitty stood just beyond the reach of the light and held her breath. The cries continued unabated. She peeked inside.

Louisa lay prostrate upon a large, fluffy bed. Head in her hands, she wept.

What happened that should affect calm, steady Louisa so profoundly? Had something befallen Mr. Bingley?

Kitty's stomach dropped, and her face turned cold. No, it could not be.

She rushed in and dropped on the bed beside Louisa. She laid her hand on Louisa's back and whispered, "Please, tell me what is wrong. Is there any way I might help?"

Louisa pushed herself up and stared at Kitty. "Oh! I am so sorry. I should not have kept you waiting. Oh my, nearly an hour now. Please, forgive me. I am so…sorry…" She covered her face again.

"Forgive me. I know I should not intrude. I have no business being in your room, but I heard you and was concerned."

Louisa peeked up, but dissolved into tears.

Kitty retrieved a handkerchief from her reticule and gave it to her.

"Thank...thank you."

"Please, can you tell me what is wrong—or at least how I may be able to help?"

"There is nothing to be done."

"Has someone been hurt or ill? Your brother? Mr. Hurst?"

"No, no, they are well."

Thank heavens! Kitty's knees barely supported her. She gripped the bedpost until they steadied. "Then what happened?"

"I just received a letter...and Charles another..."

"It contained bad news?"

"Yes." She lifted her head and looked at Kitty with eyes too much like Mama's when she learnt of Lydia's elopement. "It is awful."

"How might I be of comfort to you?"

"You cannot. We are ruined."

"How? What happened?"

"What else? What...who has always been the problem for us?"

"Caroline?"

"Yes, yes. Caroline. Once again she has had her way."

"What did she do?"

"I am not actually sure."

"But you said you are ruined."

"We are."

"Louisa, you are not making any sense. Please tell me what is going on."

"The letter I received was from Miss Hurst. She offered me condolences for what Caroline had done."

"But you have no idea what that is?" It could not be worse than Lydia's transgressions.

"No. I have no idea. It must be awful to prompt such a letter."

Kitty helped her sit up. "There is more?"

Louisa nodded and forced back yet another sob. "I suppose everyone will know soon enough."

"Will know what?"

"She said…said…she suggests that Mr. Hurst may…may not want to…"

"Marry you under the circumstances?"

"Yes, yes, exactly. Their family is…is not…in a position to weather scandal. They cannot afford to be connected with…"

"So tainted a family?"

"Yes. She has ruined everything! Everything! You must now go too, I am sure."

"Hardly. My sisters are well married. They will not be harmed by my friendship with you."

A fresh wave of sobs washed over Louisa.

"Keep in mind, you have no idea of what actually happened. It may only be rumor and conjecture after all. You know how talk spreads."

"But you know Caroline—"

"Have you spoken to Mr. Hurst?"

"No."

"Then you do not know what his response is or if there is anything at all for him to respond to."

"But—"

"You told me he regards you highly, did you not?"

She mouthed something that looked like *yes*.

"Then do not allow his sister to speak for him. What has been done to ascertain what actually happened?"

"A letter came this morning from Sir James who witnessed her disgrace. Charles has gone to see him."

"Good. If he observed the event, you should be able to have an accurate account soon. We must only wait."

"But…but…"

"No, enough of that. No more fretting until we are certain there is something genuine to fret about." She helped Louisa to her feet. "I shall call the housekeeper for tea and then a tray with a light supper—"

"Oh no! Dinner. I meant to send you word and cancel—"

"Do not bother yourself with that one whit. It seems a good thing I am here after all." Kitty pulled the bell cord. "Now, you freshen yourself up, and I will see to everything else."

The housekeeper appeared and, though startled to see Kitty, recovered admirably well. Tea and supper arrived in short order.

"I am not hungry." Louisa whispered.

Kitty urged her to the small table.

"Of course you are not, but it does not signify. You still must eat. Hunger, even if you do not recognize you are hungry, only makes one's upset worse" Kitty transferred apple sauce and cold pork to Louisa's plate. "No argument, now—eat."

Louisa screwed up her face, but took a bite. Soon she ate with dainty relish.

"You have not eaten all day, have you? You have barely stirred from your room."

Louisa swallowed hard and looked away.

"I know. Maintaining your routine is the last thing you want right now, but it is the best thing for you."

Louisa lifted her hands and shook her head.

"You may not like it, but I am right. You will see. Tomorrow morning, I will help you manage the household business, and you will be all the better for it."

"You will stay tonight?"

"Of course, I will. This is not the time for you to be alone."

Louisa threw her arms around Kitty's neck and sniffled into her shoulder. "Thank you."

"You are most welcome. As soon as we finish supper, I will send a note to my aunt and uncle. With their permission, of course, I will stay as long as you need me."

"You are the very best of friends." Louisa eased back into her chair.

Kitty smiled and urged her to eat a little more. Once finished, Kitty busied herself at Louisa's writing desk. By the time she finished, Louisa slept on her bed, curled around a pillow clutched to her stomach.

❧ Chapter 9

KITTY TIPTOED INTO THE hallway and downstairs, searching for the housekeeper who appeared wraith-like in the foyer.

"Miss Bingley is sleeping now. Leave the tray. It is best she not be disturbed."

"Right, Miss. Will you be staying the night then?"

"Yes. Have my coachman take this to the Gardiners."

"Very good, Miss. The maid will ready the guest room for you. Would you like to wait in the parlor?"

"Yes. Does Miss Bingley have a work basket? I did not bring my own."

"I will bring it shortly." The housekeeper hurried away.

Kitty slipped into the now familiar parlor and settled into a large chair near the fireplace. A maid delivered Miss Bingley's work basket. Catherine might sit primly with her hands folded in her lap, but Kitty needed to keep her fingers busy.

What a relief to leave *Catherine* behind.

A delicate muslin bodice called to her from the top of the pile. As tempting as the intricate embroidery was, the pattern was unfamiliar. Best not risk ruining it. She set it aside in favor of a man's shirt much in need of mending. She snapped the shirt open over her lap. The scent of sandalwood rose from the muslin. She swallowed hard and lifted the shirt to examine it in the firelight. The cuffs and collar were frayed and the left elbow almost worn through.

Mr. Bingley worried his collar when uneasy. He must have been attending business meetings recently. Social engagements never made him fret. He wore his sleeves a mite too long, so his cuffs were always a bit dingy and frayed. No reputable tailor would claim such shoddy work. Perhaps he inherited them from his father.

She could shorten the sleeves a touch—but for that she would have to take his measure. For now, she could start on the collar and elbow.

These were not the first repairs on this shirt. Collar and cuffs would soon need to be replaced. Either he liked it very well, or disliked visiting the tailor. Perhaps she should have a word with his valet. The man ought to pay better attention to his master's garments. She stroked the fabric. A sharp pinch in her chest forced tears to her eyes. She wiped them away with the back of her hand and began mending.

She finished the collar and elbow and jabbed her needle into the left cuff. The front door opened and weary footfalls trudged in. A moment later, Mr. Bingley appeared in the doorway, his face that of a spaniel mud-splashed by a passing carriage.

Kitty tossed the shirt aside and rushed to him. She took his hat and coat, passed them to the maid, and ordered a tray brought in. She guided him to the chair she had been using near the fire and sat on the footstool nearby.

"I did not expect you," he murmured.

"I can go upstairs, if you would rather be alone."

"No, please stay. I am glad you are here."

They watched the fire crackle and pop. The maid arrived with a tray of broth and bread. Kitty took it from her. She placed it on the table beside him.

He shook his head, tapping his fist to his lips.

"Louisa said the self-same thing. Still, you must eat something." She pressed a bowl into his hands. "Sip the broth. It will do you good."

He turned to her. What had he discovered?

Her throat clenched. "It is less effort to comply than to argue."

He closed his eyes and drank the broth. She buttered a slice of bread and gave it to him as he set the bowl down.

"You are most persistent."

"The fourth of five sisters must be if she is to receive any notice at all." She offered him a napkin. "Better now?"

He touched the napkin to his lips and handed it back to her. He held her fingers ever so briefly. "Yes."

"Was it as bad as you feared?"

He nodded very slowly. "Caroline attended a large dinner party hosted by Lord Ashton at his home in Scarborough. How she obtained an invitation is quite beyond me."

Kitty grimaced. "Oh dear."

"I told our aunt not to allow Caroline to attend social gatherings. Even under our aunt's supervision, my sister still could not control…"

"Her tongue? Her temper?"

"If only it were something so simple." He raked the hair back from his forehead. "I fear I made a serious error sending her to Scarborough."

"How so?"

"When Caroline is very unhappy she partakes in far too much wine. She says it relieves her misery."

"She imbibed too much at dinner?"

"Far too much. Sir James Bruce, an old friend of mine, attended the dinner as well. He tells me Caroline joined in too many toasts. Her words become unguarded and harsh when she is inebriated. She spoke very ill of Darcy, Mrs. Darcy and the entire house of Matlock."

"All of whom had friends in attendance?"

"Indeed." He clutched his temples. "If that were not enough, she tripped over the edge of a carpet as they withdrew, ladies and gentlemen together. She fell into Lord Ashton's son, and her gown ripped when he caught her."

"Oh, no." Kitty screwed her eyes shut and bit her lip.

"Caroline considered herself compromised and insisted Ashton's son must marry her. Quite forcefully, as I understand."

"Surely the words of an intoxicated woman are not to be taken seriously. They cannot be held against you."

He pinched his temples. "Scarborough has not so many opportunities for scandal as London. The story has taken on a life of its own and shall haunt her all of her days."

"I understand."

"How ironic the one time Caroline is not actively trying to promote her ambitions—that is the time she throws us into ruin." He rose and went to the fireplace. One hand on the mantle, he nudged the fire with the poker. "This will be in the scandal sheets, much magnified I am certain. Soon Louisa and I will be ruined. I do not believe Hurst will stand with her."

"She told me. Do you think him so inconstant?"

He exhaled heavily. "He is influenced by his sister. She wants him to marry a gentleman's daughter. He has an acceptable excuse—"

"Louisa will be devastated."

"I cannot protect her. I have failed."

"I understand how—"

He spun on his heel and stared at her. "You must go. Association with us will only damage you."

"But—"

"No. You must go."

"I do not need to—"

He glowered and pointed toward the door.

How could he turn her away when she was ready to stand with him? She regretted her supper, now churning acidly in her belly.

"Did you hear me?"

"I did."

"Then do as I ask!" he growled through gritted teeth.

"I do not think—"

"This is the only way to protect you. I insist you allow me to do that. Do as I ask, now."

She shrugged, swallowing the acrid tang coating the back of her tongue. Her hand shook as she picked up his shirt from the mending pile. "Your cuffs wear because your sleeves are too long. You need to find a better tailor." She shoved the shirt into his hands and left.

She forced herself toward the stairs, barely able to breathe. The heavy air weighed upon her, suffocating. Each step felt like three, her feet too full of stone to lift.

At last in the guest room, she crumpled to the floor and leaned against the neat oak bedpost, the wood as cold and hard as his words.

Why would he be that way? There was no need. She knew their pain too well. A unique gaping wound when everything had been ripped away by the fault or action of another, and nothing one could do might redeem it.

She wrapped her arms around her knees, and hid her face. Empty shivers coursed down her back and arms. If only she might comfort Louisa. She could comfort them both, if permitted. Why would he deny her?

Stubborn, vexing man! Mr. Richards was entirely wrong—brothers, men—were far more trying than women. Why would he not listen?

She ground her teeth, clenched fists shoved into her ribs. How brutally unfair! She pushed to her feet and paced in the wane moonlight, her chest stuffed so full of conflicting feelings, she could hardly draw breath.

He said he did not want her here. She should go back to the Gardiners where she might be surrounded by a loving family and make herself useful. Why should she fight him?

Because she loved her friends and…

Enough! She would not turn her back on her friends, even if they demanded it. *Kitty* Bennet was made of far sterner stuff.

She stalked downstairs.

Mr. Bingley still stood at the fireplace, arms against the mantle, head bowed. "What are you doing here?"

"Standing with my friends."

"Did I not tell you to go? Quit all association with us before it is too late."

She strode in, shoulders squared, chin high.

"You do not know what you are about."

"How would you know what I am about when you will not listen to me?"

He dropped the poker. It clattered a loud protest. "I told you, go."

"I do not wish to. I choose to stay."

"I…I…do not want you here."

She gazed into his weary eyes. Those were not the eyes of one who wanted to be alone. She stood a little straighter.

He inched closer and licked his lips. For an instant, his eyes softened, but he pulled away as quickly. "You should not be here. It is improper. Go now."

She stomped closer to him and crossed her arms over her chest. "No."

He leaned down, his breath hot on her face. "Get out. Now." He pointed to the door, arm quivering.

"You do not mean that."

"You presume to know my own mind for me? Presumptuous chit! "

"I know more than you think." She flashed a quick, tight smile.

"Perhaps—"

"I am tired of allowing others to determine the means by which I may be happy and will stand for it no more." Her heart throbbed in her ears. "You cannot choose with whom I will associate. No one but I can do that."

"You…you are…a stupid, ignorant, silly girl."

"Calling me names and insulting me is your means of protecting me?" She pumped her fists at her side and snorted. "You look ridiculous when you try to ape Mr. Darcy. You do it poorly and it does not become you."

"You mock me?"

"What do you expect? You are behaving like a petulant little boy not even breeched! Shall I take your leading strings?"

Veins in his neck and forehead pulsated. "Now you insult me as you judge me?"

"No. I am a victim of judgment as much as you."

"What do you know of the pain of judgment or being outcast?"

"Far more than you believe."

"Your words are very brave but entirely uninformed." He waved his finger in her face. "I must protect you better than I have Louisa."

"I did not ask for your protection."

"Obstinate, headstrong—"

"—and right. I am right."

"Do you understand? Caroline has cost me everything…everything I have ever hoped for." He stared deep into her eyes.

She grabbed his finger and forced it away. "You are not the only one to suffer loss."

"How? Did one of your pretty little friends—"

"You beastly, arrogant, horrible fop." Her hand flew.

The sharp crack against his cheek echoed in the dim room.

She leaned so close their noses almost touched. "You do not even know what it is like. This to-do with Caroline still may come to nothing. It is still all conjecture. If anyone here appreciates what rejection and isolation is like, it is me."

Mr. Bingley rolled his eyes and tossed his head. "Everyone is paying more attention to your younger sister than you?"

"How dare you! How dare you!" Her voice thinned to a razor sharp shriek. "Were you not listening? Lydia eloped a month after Lizzy and Jane married, leaving me an outcast for nigh on six months."

He gaped at her, unblinking, unmoving.

"No one beyond Longbourn has spoken to me for months. People look away when I walk past—my friends cross the street to avoid me!"

His jaw worked, but no words came forth.

"There, you have it now. I am the pariah, not you. You should be far more concerned with what your association with *me* might cost *you*. I am ruined...you can do me no further harm." Her throat burned.

The truth was fully out; its power no longer sustained her. She sagged against the mantle.

His brows knit as though he struggled to work out what she had said. Could he really be so stupid?

She dug her nails into her palms. "This is the first company I have kept since summer! Now you are throwing me out, too. Little matter, I am quite used to it by now. I will be gone at first light, unless, of course, you insist I go now." She spun on her heel and marched out.

Her bravado shattered at the foot of the stairs. She dashed up, blinded by the sandy burning in her eyes. She paused at the top, gasping for breath as though laced in her grandmother's corset. It would be a relief to cry, but that was not going to happen—not now, not ever again. She tried to take a step toward her room, but found she still clutched the banister.

A presence rose behind her. She ran. After only three paces, a firm grip on her shoulder stopped her.

"Stop—please. Wait." The voice, Mr. Bingley's, was soft as blue velvet.

She turned, still shaking.

The moonlight through the window painted his profile with cold silvery brightness. The sharp edges to his countenance had melted way, leaving something gentle and vulnerable behind. This was the man she knew and—

"I had no idea. Why did you not tell me?"

She shrugged and turned her face aside. "You hardly think it the kind of thing one would freely announce at tea. 'Oh, by the by, my sister utterly ruined my family—just thought you ought to know.'"

He coughed a small laugh. "I suppose it would hardly do." He tipped her chin up. "I believe all the etiquette manuals eschew scandal as an appropriate topic of conversation."

"We must wholly apply ourselves to follow their sage advice. " She never had been good at play acting. It rang clear in her voice. Little matter now.

"Indeed." He met her gaze, his palm cradling her cheek. "I am so sorry. I cannot imagine how awful...all these months...I regret Louisa and I were unable to stay at Netherfield—"

All the anguish she had woven together into a melancholy cloak unraveled. Her knees buckled, and she hid her face in her hands. Waves of hysterical sobs tore from her throat.

Warm, strong arms smelling of sandalwood and mint surrounded her, supported her, comforted her. A cool linen square pressed into her hand.

She held it to her eyes and hiccupped back the last of her cries. "Forgive me," her whisper rasped so hoarse she barely recognized her own voice. "I should not have—"

One arm still tight about her, he lifted her chin with the other hand. "What untrue things did you say? What did you do that I did not deserve?"

"But I—"

"Granted," he touched his cheek, "I do not prefer you to continue to use that particular device to garner my attention. In this case, though, I think it may be deserved."

"I should go." She willed herself to pull way. Her limbs barely cooperated.

"No." He pulled her close and pressed her head to his chest. "No, you should not."

"But I...this is—"

"Exactly as it should be."

His heart beat beneath her ear, strong and reassuring. Everything about this situation was wrong.

Alone, in the dark, she in his arms, the situation befitted Lydia or Caroline. "I must—"

"Marry me."

She froze. "What did you say?"

"You must marry me."

"How can you say that? A moment ago you demanded I leave."

"You must believe me very impulsive"

"Mad was the word that came to my mind. Perhaps I should have fashioned your shirt into a straight-waistcoat to wear on your trip to Bedlam."

He laughed and drew his fingertips along her jaw. "I assure you, this is not madness. I have thought this through very well, even talked with Darcy about it—at length."

"I did not know he was given to long discussions. I thought my brother quite spare of words." Her eyebrows twitched up.

His lips pressed into the most inviting smile. "I never regretted anything as much as our departure from Netherfield. I intended to court you properly at Pemberley whilst we visited and finally set all things to rights." His arms tightened briefly. "Nothing has truly been right since we left."

She blinked several times. Certainly she would awake from this dream in just a moment. But Mr. Bingley remained resolutely in focus.

"You do not believe me?"

"I...I hardly know what to think."

"I suppose I can understand that well enough." He stroked her cheek with the side of his finger. "You still have not given me an answer."

"You are serious?"

"Absolutely. Thoughts of you distract me constantly. I can hardy draw breath without pining for the fragrance of your perfume. My greatest loss was when Louisa left to visit the Hursts, and she no longer read me your delightful letters. Those letters made me feel I was still close to you. Without them, I was bereft."

"I missed you." She swallowed hard. "I scarcely allowed myself to believe you might feel the same. After Lydia...I was certain you would not want—"

He dropped to one knee and pressed his lips to her hand. "Miss Kitty Bennet—would you end my suffering and consent to be my wife?"

She squeaked something that must have sounded like 'yes', because he jumped to his feet and gathered her into his arms. Their lips met and lingered in exquisite warmth. Tears poured down her cheeks in rivulets that rippled with the pounding of her heart.

He tried to brush them away with his thumbs. "These are the happy kind?"

She nodded.

He licked his lips.

Might he kiss her again? Was it wrong to hope he would?

Someone gasped.

They turned. Louisa stood at the end of the corridor, silhouetted in the moonlight, covering her mouth with her hands.

"Oh! I...we..." Kitty tried to jump away, but he held her fast to him.

Bingley beckoned Louisa.

"You heard everything?" Kitty squeaked.

Louisa bobbed her head. "I had no idea of what happened in Meryton. Why did you not tell me?"

Kitty shrugged, eyes burning again. "Do you want to talk about Caroline?"

"I suppose not."

"She is going to marry me." Mr. Bingley—her Mr. Bingley pulled her closer. A brilliant smile lit his face.

"My reputation may give Mr. Hurst further reason—"

"I rather have a sister who will stand by me than a man who will not." Louisa cuffed his shoulder. "It is time you finally did this."

He snorted and glowered briefly, but it turned into a snicker. "You are quite correct."

Kitty woke in a strange bed to sandy eyes and a scratchy throat. A hot drink was definitely in order. She pushed the counterpane aside and slid out of bed. Louisa's dressing gown fell awkwardly across her back, shoulders too narrow and bodice too long.

How they giggled and chattered in the wee hours of the morning. She hugged herself. Louisa was almost as happy as she.

She slipped her dress on. The gown still smelled faintly of Bingley. The man she preferred above all others had indeed asked for her hand. He had kissed her and embraced her and they would be married! Light feet carried her to the breakfast room where the fragrance of chocolate and warm toast greeted her.

"Good morning, my princess." Bingley's smile outshone the morning sunshine. He pulled out the chair beside his. "Sit with me. I ordered a pot of chocolate especially for you this morning." He kissed her hand and brought the silver chocolate pot close and spun the chocolate mill in his palms. "I like generous foam on my chocolate. I hope you agree."

"I do." She tittered as he poured her cup.

"What? Am I doing something wrong?"

"A gentleman has never served me chocolate before."

"You must simply accustom yourself to it." He winked and sipped his cup. "Perhaps a touch too much pepper this morning. We will find our particular blend of spices."

"I like the sound of that."

He placed his chocolate cup within the delicate rails of the saucer. "We should go to your uncle this morning. I must seek his approval."

"I am sure he will grant it. After all, Aunt Gardiner thinks highly of you. He will insist we go to Papa, though."

"I expected as much." He offered her the platter of toast and took several slices himself. "I will be honest with them about Caroline."

"Of course, you must."

"You do not fear they will deny us?"

She laughed, but it left a bitter trace on her tongue. "Papa will be glad someone of quality will still have me. He will be relieved for you to take me off his hands."

"Do not say such things."

"Why not? It is true."

"I do not care whether it is true or not. I have no desire to hear you say such things about the woman I love."

She gasped and pressed her fist to her mouth.

"You think far too meanly of yourself. I will not have it continue. You must regard yourself as highly as I do." He gazed at her. Who knew blue eyes could hold such fire?

"I…I…I think it may be difficult." Oh, dear! It was good she was already sitting—too much of that expression he wore would surely melt her knees.

Mr. Darcy looked at Lizzy that way. No wonder she could scarcely resist him.

"Then I shall help! We shall hire the Meryton Assembly rooms and host a party—a ball for Twelfth Night."

"You cannot prepare for a ball in merely week! Besides, Mama has already sent invitations for Longbourn's traditional Twelfth Night party. Papa insisted she go through with it though she fears few will come."

"Even better. We will make it known in town that Louisa and I have come especially for the occasion. That should incite curiosity and increase attendance. It may be the last event we enjoy before Caroline's behavior becomes common knowledge. Best we use the opportunity to please your mother."

"A party?" Louisa peeked in.

"Yes, we have a splendid notion—to attend Longbourn's Twelfth Night party. What better way to announce our engagement?" Bingley said.

"How marvelous! When shall we leave? I can pack very quickly."

"We will see the Gardiners directly. While my dear Kitty—"

She blushed. How well her name sounded on his lips.

"—packs, I will handle a few spots of business. We can be off by afternoon. If you do not object to taking a meal in the carriage, we may be in Meryton by evening tonight!"

"You are right. It is a good plan!" Louisa made up a plate of toast and poured chocolate. "I shall pack immediately." She hurried off, breakfast in hand.

"Do you always do things this way?"

"More or less."

"How is it you and Mr. Darcy are such good friends?"

"We complement each other well." He shrugged. "Are you pleased with these arrangements?"

"Yes, I suppose so. I have hardly had time to consider." She bit her lip and struggled not to bounce in her seat. "Yes, it sounds delightful."

"Let us be off to your uncle's. We have a great deal to accomplish."

<hr/>

Aunt greeted them at the door, not looking nearly as surprised as she should.

"Good morning. Oh, we have had such a night. I am sure you cannot even imagine. There is so much to tell. I must pack for we are going back to Meryton today. We will be there by evening. Mama and Papa will be so surprised. I dare say Mama will be most pleased."

Aunt took Kitty's wrap. "You may find it helpful to take a breath now and again, dear. No one is going to interrupt you."

Kitty's face flushed. "I am sorry. I hardly know what I am saying."

"Please, madam," Bingley removed his hat. "Is your husband available? May I speak to him?"

"It is a good thing you are so early as he has not yet left for the day. He is in his study." Aunt nodded to the housekeeper who hovered close. She ushered Bingley down the hall.

Aunt took Kitty by the elbow, hurried her to the morning room and shut the door. "So tell me."

"You were right, he does not care—he has never cared about those things, except of course when his sister—who is quite horrible—does them. Then it vexes him most seriously."

Aunt slid into the closest chair. "Perhaps you should begin this story at the beginning."

Kitty dropped into the chair beside her and drew a deep breath. She related the events of the previous evening only gasping for air once during the entire recitation. When she caught her breath, she added, "Oh, will Uncle approve? Will he let me go to Meryton today? Louisa will be riding with us so we will have a proper chaperone. What will Papa say? Do you think—"

Aunt took Kitty's hand. "Shhh—calm yourself."

"How can I possibly calm myself when everything—"

"—will be fine? I wrote your father the day we first encountered Mr. Bingley. I told him of my suspicions, so this will not come as a shock, although this trip seems a bit poorly planned."

"I expect they wish to be away from here as much as I did Meryton."

"How do you feel about returning?"

"I hate it—but we must, at the very least for Mama and Papa's approval. I am sure we can go to Pemberley and be married from there. Mr. Pierce would certainly do it for us."

"And then what? Where will you live?"

"I suppose we will come back to his townhouse. By then we will discern the reach of Caroline's scandal and the steadfastness of Mr. Hurst. If things are well, we can stay. If not, he still desires to take a country home. If not the estate near Derby that Mr. Darcy recommends, we will find a place, between here and Pemberley, perhaps Leicester or North Hampton, where we are not so difficult a distance from any of you.

"That seems quite reasonable. Shall I help you pack?"

Kitty blinked and pulled back. "You are not going to ask me if I am not being too impulsive, if I know him well enough or am ready for this step? You are not concerned I am simply fleeing my problems in Meryton or just trading them for the problems Caroline is causing? You do not fear I am adding another terrible sister to the one I already have?"

"No."

"But...but why? I thought you would at least be concerned—"

"My dear girl, cannot you see? I do not need to ask those things because I can see you have."

"Oh."

"You are not the flighty, unreasonable a girl you have been led to believe yourself to be. I am entirely convinced, Kitty Bennet, you are entirely sufficient to this endeavor."

By the time they left the morning room, Bingley had already departed with a promise to return in several hours. Uncle set to penning a letter for her to deliver to her father while she, Aunt and Alice packed her trunks. They were much more pleasant help than Hill and Mattie.

Her trunks were waiting in the foyer when the Bingley carriage arrived. The driver quickly loaded them while she kissed her cousins goodbye. Aunt pressed a filled hamper into her hands. Uncle handed her into the coach, and they were off.

Kitty set the hamper on the floor and arranged her skirts. "I do not know why Aunt insisted on this. She said it was just in case—"

Louisa giggled, covered her mouth with both hands, and laughed harder.

Bingley slapped his forehead. "I knew I forgot something."

"Aunt did think you a bit distracted." Kitty rolled her eyes. "Did you have much to attend to this morning?"

"He has been flitting about like a sparrow in a freshly sown garden. How many letters did you dash off before we left?"

"Not that many."

"I wonder any of them are legible with you flying from one meeting to the next before and after you wrote."

"You portray me as some kind of simpleton."

"Hardly, brother. Truthfully, you amaze me with your ability to get things done very quickly when you put your mind to it."

"He is as efficient as my brother Darcy then?"

"Perhaps not quite that much, but once Charles's mind is made up, little will stop him."

"Now you make it sound as though I will not listen to good counsel."

"Not at all! Why are you so determined to hear insult? I mean only admiration. I know none else who can put a plan into action as quickly as you."

Kitty smiled and batted her eyes at him. "Perhaps because he has a great deal of practice following through on the impulse of the moment."

"Now you mean to flatter me and appeal to my vanity? What am I to do with either of you?" He glanced from Louisa to Kitty, his face formed into shapes of exasperation, but his eyes glittered.

✥ Chapter 10

BINGLEY'S ESTIMATE PROVED optimistic. Afternoon waxed and waned into evening then night before the coach pulled up to Longbourn house.

Kitty hesitated at the door. Ordinarily, she would have walked in without a second thought. Tonight was not remotely ordinary.

Bingley poised to knock and glanced at her.

"Please," she whispered.

He rapped sharply. Kitty counted fluttering heartbeats until the door peeked open. Hill gasped and swung it wide.

"Miss Kitty?"

"I am well, do not fear." Kitty took the housekeeper's weathered hands and patted them. "We have a most delightful surprise." She led them past Hill who seemed rooted in place.

Halfway through the foyer, Hill regained herself and rushed to them. "I...I...shall I get the Master? Shall I send something to eat?"

"A tray in the parlor whilst we await Papa would be delightful."

"Yes, Miss." Hill curtsied but teetered on the way down.

Bingley caught her arm. "There now, do not be uneasy. Truly, everything is well."

"Yes, sir." Hill brushed her hands down her apron and hurried off.

"I fear we gave her quite a shock." Bingley followed Kitty into the parlor.

"This is a shocking time for callers to arrive." Louisa unwound her shawl and draped it over her arm.

"Hill has been most unsettled since—" Kitty bit her lip, "—since Lydia. The whole household has."

Louisa squeezed her hand and sat beside her on the settee. "I understand."

"I know you do." Kitty forced a smile.

"No talk of such dark subjects when we gather for the happiest of reasons." Bingley gave his jacket a sharp tug.

"And what would that be?" Papa stood silhouetted in the doorway, arms crossed tightly over his chest. "I saw you off to Darcy House and presumed you would be on your way to Pemberley by now. I cannot fathom why you—and your friends are here."

Kitty dashed to his side. "Are you not pleased to see me?" Her insides quivered like one of Cook's tapioca jellies. If only Lizzy were here. She alone could accurately divine Papa's glances from his glares.

The creases around his eyes softened just a bit. "I am not displeased to see you. I simply wish to comprehend what brought you here, at this hour, with no letter to presage your arrival."

"It was all rather sudden, really." Kitty said.

"Quite sudden." Louisa nodded.

"Obviously."

"Perhaps I might be able to explain." Bingley stood before him, shoulders square, jaw firm, more handsome than Kitty had ever seen him. Considering his normal dashing—

"Is that so? I am sure it will be quite the explanation."

"Would you grant me an interview in private, sir?"

Papa's eyebrows climbed high, almost touching his hair. He looked at Kitty.

She pressed her lips tightly and barely nodded. "Uncle sent this letter for you." She handed it to him.

"Very well, then." Papa took the missive and ushered Bingley out.

A moment later, Hill bustled in with a tray. "Will this do, Miss?"

"It is lovely." Kitty took the tray. "You should go and attend Mama. I expect she will want to come downstairs."

Hill peeked over her shoulder toward Papa's study. "That is a very good thing." She curtsied and dashed off.

"Do you think your father will be pleased?" Louisa asked.

Kitty shrugged and busied herself making tea. Her fingers were thick and clumsy on the lid of the tea caddy. She nearly spilled leaves on the table in her attempts to spoon them out.

"Thank you." Louisa took the tea cup. "Do not be anxious. It will be fine. I am sure."

"Oh, you do not know Papa. He can be so very contrary. Just when you expect him to go one way, he goes another—only, it seems, to vex us all. He would not heed Lizzy's warnings about Lydia and—" Her throat constricted and strangled the remainder of her speech. Not that it needed to be said. Louisa knew well enough.

"He will not become stubborn now, especially because it will make your mother so happy."

"He always tries to keep her happy. Perhaps you are right."

"Of course I am. Now, as you told me not long ago, eat something. It will not do for you to face all this excitement hungry and cross." Louisa piled slices of bread, cheese and meat on a small plate and pushed it into Kitty's hand.

"You are a very bossy sister."

"I assure you, it is a new experience for me, and I am going to like it very well indeed."

Kitty nibbled on the bread. "I think it unfair. It should be my turn to be the bossy one now."

"Shall we take turns? Yesterday, it was your turn. Today, it is mine. Tomorrow, I promise, it will be yours again."

"Oh, very well." Kitty harrumphed and giggled under her breath.

"That is much better."

Heavy foot falls rang out in the corridor. Fuzzy prickles scoured her face whilst an angry cat chased its tail in her belly. How slowly could they walk? Oh bother, would they not end her suffering?

Bingley strode in first, beaming more broadly than she had ever seen.

Air flooded her lungs so fast flickers of light blocked her vision. She flung out her hand and grabbed for the arm of the settee.

"Had the Gardiners not written and prepared me for this possibility, I would be most surprised indeed." Papa thumbed his lapels.

"Papa?" Her voice was only a squeak, an annoying little girl squeak at that.

"Yes, yes, dear. I could hardly fail to offer my approbation—"

"Thank you!" She flew across the room and hugged him.

He patted her back, a bit awkwardly, but it was reassuring nonetheless.

"I suppose I should go upstairs and inform your mother of this felicitous turn of events. I expect she will be rather more excited about her Twelfth Night party now." He looked at Bingley with an odd glint in his eye.

"I believe you are quite correct." Bingley winked.

Papa shambled out.

Appetizing aromas wafted from the tray, seasoned by Bingley's infectious laughter. The candles flickered more brightly. They settled in to enjoy food, company and a most comfortable room.

An hour later, Papa appeared, Mama on his arm.

"Mama!"

"Mrs. Bennet." Bingley rose and bowed. Beside him, Louisa curtsied.

"You are most welcome, sir. I hope you and your good sister will stay at Longbourn with us." Mama's voice trembled, and her complexion resembled foolscap, but her fragile smile was entirely genuine, the first one in months.

"Thank you most kindly."

"When you are finished, Hill will show you to your rooms. Tomorrow, Kitty, I will need your help. Additional plans for Twelfth Night must be made."

"Yes…certainly, Mama."

"Enjoy yourselves, dears. I shall go speak to Hill." She patted Papa's arm.

"Let us find her then." Papa smiled at her. The shadows under his eyes had faded, and his lips curved up just a little. They disappeared into the hall.

Louisa grabbed her hand. "You see, I told you. You had nothing to fear."

Kitty tucked a stray lock of hair behind her ear. "I am all astonishment."

"Perhaps next time, you will listen to me."

"Yes, I suppose. But tomorrow, it will be my turn to be the bossy older sister."

She awoke in her old bed. A familiar ray of sun tugged at her eyelids. She rushed through her morning ablutions and threw on a plain morning dress. A quick peek in the mirror and she thought better of it. Mr. Bingley was here, after all.

She changed into a pretty gown, one with hard to reach buttons down the back. She won a protracted struggle with her buttons and hurried downstairs.

Muffled voices led her to the morning room where Louisa, Mama and Mr. Bingley sat, hunched low over one of Mama's books.

"Good morning, Kitty dear." Mama turned a page and smoothed her fingertips along the fresh sheet. Her pencil scratched across the page.

Kitty sat and leaned in to examine Mama's neat curls and loops.

"We have been going over…menus for the party."

"Menus? You decided upon those well before I left."

"Yes, yes…"

"But gracious hostess that she is, she wanted to consult us on our favorites." Louisa glanced at Bingley.

"You know how much I favor Longbourn's carrot soup." Bingley rose and pulled out a chair for Kitty.

"I will need you to go into town to place several new orders. We shall need a larger Twelfth Night cake now."

Mama's hand still quivered, and her voice was weak. But she was dressed and out of her room for the first time in months. Who would have imagined it possible?

"Louisa, would you care to accompany me when I go to town?"

"I would be delighted," Louisa said.

"Might I join you as well?" Bingley beamed. "I have business there. I would be proud to escort the two prettiest girls in the county."

Kitty blushed. Should she enjoy his compliments and attention so much? "I think it a lovely idea."

Not an hour later, the three were on their way to Meryton. As the first buildings of town rose up before them, Kitty braced herself for sidelong stares and turned backs. At least in the company of the Bingleys, she would not be so entirely alone.

"What say you, shall we stop for chocolate after we finish our business?" Bingley asked.

After her last visit, she hesitated to venture to the coffee house again. But Bingley's eyes— "Very well."

"Capital." He ushered them into the chandler's shop and promised to meet them soon at the coffee house.

The shopkeeper remembered Louisa from their time at Netherfield and struck up a conversation that soon included Kitty. Other shopkeepers seemed friendlier as well. Though some still turned aside, fewer people looked at her askance.

"Kitty! Miss Bingley?"

Kitty spun around. Charlotte and Maria approached.

"We did not know you had returned. I thought you visiting Lizzy for Twelfth Night," Charlotte said.

"When you left, we were sure your mother would cancel the party with you gone." Maria clasped her hands below her chin.

"We came to Meryton for Longbourn's Twelfth Night Party." Louisa winked at Kitty.

"It certainly has not been canceled." Kitty winked back. "What is more, Mama sent us to order a larger cake for the evening."

Maria's eyes widened. "Longbourn's parties are always memorable. It is hard to imagine Twelfth Night without one."

"You will come, then?" Kitty asked.

Maria glanced at Charlotte who smiled and nodded. "I am sure we will."

"You are looking very well, Kitty." Charlotte stared at her. "Is that a new bonnet or perhaps a new pelisse?"

"No, they are not, but I have a lovely new gown for the party." Kitty shrugged.

"Come, Maria, we should leave Kitty to her company." Charlotte's gaze drifted over Kitty's shoulder. "Besides, Mama will surely want to know that Longbourn will be hosting guests for Twelfth Night."

"Yes, she will be very pleased!" Maria hurried off.

Charlotte blinked slowly and shook her head. "Good day, Miss Bingley, Mr. Bingley." She grabbed Kitty's hands and kissed her cheek. "You really do look splendid." She strode after her sister.

"Chocolate?" Bingley gestured toward the door.

"Absolutely." Kitty's feet barely grazed the polished wood floors as she walked in.

The following days overflowed with frenzied party preparations. Mr. Bingley spent his days either ensconced in the study with Papa or in numerous unnamed errands to Meryton. Probably best that way, all told. Mama still spent many hours resting but provided daily lists for Kitty and Louisa who managed the bulk of the work.

At least they were finally receiving responses to their invitation. Few directly declined, yet less than half accepted outright. Hopefully, Mama would not be too disappointed.

The sun sank into the horizon, and all was in readiness for the Twelfth Night party. Hill lit the final candles as Kitty made her descent down a staircase trimmed with evergreen and holly. The smells of Twelfth Night swirled around her, inviting her to join their dance.

"How wonderful you look! Is that the dress your sisters gave you?" Mrs. Bennet fluttered about the base of the stairs.

"It is." Kitty looked past Mama to Bingley who stared at her, a little slacked jaw. "I have your approval?"

Bingley nodded. He did not appear as though he could speak.

Mama stepped close and took her hand. "I can hardly imagine anything finer. The trims on the skirt are exquisite and your turban—"

"I am glad you like it. I do believe I am much happier wearing it here than at the earl's for Christmas dinner."

"Nonsense, child! It is such a shame you missed the opportunity."

Papa bustled up and took Mama's elbow. "We should go to the foyer. Our guests are arriving."

Kitty followed them and took her place beside her mother. How strange to stand where Jane and Elizabeth always had. Bingley and Louisa smiled at her from the parlor door.

The front door creaked open to admit muffled voices and shuffling wraps. Hill ushered in the first arrivals.

"Lizzy?" Kitty's jaw dropped.

"How well you look, my dear Mrs. Darcy!" Mama grabbed Lizzy's hands and kissed her cheeks. "You have been taking very good care of my dear girl. Have you not, Mr. Darcy?"

"It is my chiefest pleasure." Mr. Darcy bowed from his shoulders, the barest corner of his lips turning up. "You seem surprised to see us, Miss Kitty." His gaze drifted over her shoulder.

"Completely, utterly surprised." She glanced over her shoulder and caught Bingley's wink at Mr. Darcy. "Did he—"

Mr. Darcy only cocked his eyebrow and tipped his head. He moved aside. Miss Darcy appeared and offered Kitty a shy smile.

"Mrs. Hartwell gave us notice a few days ago. She is engaged." Lizzy's eyebrows rose.

Kitty bit her lip and nodded. Doubtless there would be a long sisterly talk to come. What a lovely thought! Perhaps Mama's titter-mice might gather tonight.

"Georgiana is coming home with us," Lizzy said.

"I am glad to see you, Miss Darcy." Kitty curtsied.

"I am pleased to be allowed to come and even gladder to be going to Pemberley." She glanced over her shoulder at her brother. "Your hat is very becoming, though I still like the stovepipe shape."

Kitty chuckled.

Miss Darcy followed her brother to the parlor.

"I think this all worked out for the best. I fear Mrs. Hartwell may have been a bit too strict. It would not do to crush Georgiana's spirit. Perhaps Mr. Bradley and I will enjoy greater success with her."

"I think it very likely." She squeezed Lizzy's hand and turned to the next pair of guests. "Mary? Mr. Pierce?"

Mary's smile gleamed. How well married life suited her.

"Did Mr. Bingley—"

"Yes." Mary kissed her cheek. "Congratulations. He is a fine match for you."

"You cannot keep her all to yourself." Jane scolded in a voice sweet as treacle.

"You too?" Kitty gulped back the lump in her throat. Col. Fitzwilliam stood just behind her. "I thought you were at Pemberley."

"We all came to Longbourn instead. Mama's parties are not to be missed."

"But did not Lizzy—"

"There will be other years for that. I expect you will not have another Twelfth Night as Miss Bennet at Longbourn."

She grabbed Jane's hand. "I am so happy to see you."

"Now, now, there will be time for all your prattle later. You cannot hold up the line." Mama tapped Kitty's shoulder.

Kitty released Jane and smoothed her dress, blinking rapidly to ease the sting in her eyes.

Aunt and Uncle Philips arrived next, followed by the Gardiners.

Uncle laughed at her utterly speechless state. "Alice and Margaret were just as mute when we told them they might attend tonight."

"You are quite their favorite cousin now." Aunt squeezed her hand.

Denizens of Meryton trickled in: Lucases, Longs, Gouldings and other faces that blended together. It no longer mattered how many of them came. She was surrounded by all those whom she loved best. No better company could be had.

The flow of guests dwindled. Mama swished her skirts—her signal that it was time to move to the parlor.

Kitty found Bingley waiting by the doorway. He offered her his arm.

"Are you pleased?" He wore the same hopeful look as Papa's hound.

"Pleased and stunned and astounded. How did you manage such a thing?"

"I told you. He accomplishes amazing things in a short order when he puts his mind to it." Louisa peeked over his shoulder. "It was so hard to keep the secret."

"Well, you were most effective. I have never been so surprised in all my life."

Bingley winked at Louisa.

"Whatever gave you the idea to do it?"

"I could not abide your final memories of Longbourn and Meryton being grim ones." He smiled so broadly the candlelight glinted off his teeth.

The glittering flashes fuzzed as her eyes filled.

He placed his warm hand over hers. "Is something wrong?"

Louisa pressed a handkerchief into Kitty's fingers.

"No, not at all. I am too pleased for words." She dabbed her cheeks and nodded vigorously.

The tinkling of a silver bell danced through the room. The noisy buzz dropped to shuffles and a few rumbling whispers.

"Welcome to Longbourn." Papa stood at the front of the room, Mama at his side.

"It is so lovely to share Twelfth Night with you, our family and friends." She leaned heavily on his arm, her voice faint. Though not her prior self yet, Mama's change was a Twelfth Night miracle indeed.

"We have particular reason to celebrate tonight." Papa looked directly at Kitty. "Our daughter, Kitty, recently became betrothed to Mr. Bingley."

Gasps, squeals, applause, and possibly a few jealous looks filled the room. All those nearest her seemed to press in at once to offer congratulations.

"As our guests of honor, they shall pick characters first tonight. Come here and choose for we shall have no games, nor music, nor dancing—"

"—nor dinner!" Col. Fitzwilliam cried.

Jane gasped and clutched his arm, her eyes twinkling.

Papa snickered. "Indeed, nor dinner, until our characters are chosen."

Bingley guided Kitty through the parting crowd. Mama held out a beaded velvet bag. Kitty reached in and removed a small card in an envelope and handed it to Papa. Bingley drew a card from Papa's hat.

Papa opened the envelopes and chuckled. "How very fitting! Meet your King and Queen for the evening."

Surely this did not occur by chance alone, but no one balked. This must be Bingley's doing as well. Mama produced gold paper crowns and placed them on their heads.

"What is your first order, my liege?" Papa bowed.

"To finish assigning characters, of course!" Bingley opened his arms to the crowd.

"And then?"

They all turned to Kitty.

"I should very much like to dance a few sets."

"Your king and queen have spoken." Papa called. "Come take your roles, and we shall dance."

Kitty and Bingley stepped back slightly behind Mama. Each guest took a character and bowed or curtsied to the evening's royalty.

Poor Mr. Darcy looked decidedly miserable until his character was revealed as Judge Solomon. How fitting and what a relief. It would not be fair for him to suffer on a night made for fun and merriment. Mr.

Pierce drew Bishop Blather and Col. Fitzwilliam Joe Giber, the King's jester, which seemed to satisfy him quite well, too well perhaps.

Margaret sidled up to her and whispered, "You look just like a princess today, Kitty." She curtsied and toppled over.

Bingley helped her to her feet.

"I am Clara Clumsy tonight? Did I do it right?" Margaret giggled.

"Perfectly dear." Kitty kissed her cheek.

"Now our sovereigns have ordered there be dancing. So, let there be." Papa gestured Kitty and Bingley to the center of the room.

"A country dance, please." Kitty looked at Mary who already sat at the pianoforte. "Sir William, would you be so good as to call the dance for us."

"I would be happy to oblige." He rumbled, smiling. Sir William always served as Master of Ceremonies at the Meryton Assembly. Though he was Joseph Rag-a-muffin tonight, it would not feel right without him at the top of the room. "What dance would you like?"

She whispered in his ear.

"The Queen wishes for 'Mutual Love'."

The coupled formed up behind Kitty and Bingley. Mary played the opening chord.

Mr. Bingley was such an accomplished partner! His steps were light, smile ready and sense of timing impeccable. Even better—now they were engaged, she may enjoy his partnership all evening.

Would there ever be such a wonderful Twelfth Night?

Mary insisted Miss Goulding play the next dance. Kitty selected a jig, which Miss Goulding could play exceptionally well.

Two further dances and King Bingley declared himself quite winded and in need of some other form of entertainment.

"What think you, my Queen?" Bingley asked, loud enough for the room to hear. "I believe a skit would be just the thing now."

""Oh yes, do!" Louisa clapped.

"Please cousin—I love a skit." Alice pressed in close, eyes pleading.

"Very well, a skit—and then supper."

A cheer rose.

"What skit does the king wish performed?" Col. Fitzwilliam asked, bowing from the waist. Even without a red coat, he cut a fine figure. No wonder Jane found him appealing.

Bingley stroked his chin and looked at the ceiling. "Now that is an excellent question. It must be something quite merry, as befitting the occasion, yet something familiar so as not to tax our tired courtiers."

"The King should stop his blithering and choose something before his weary courtiers all fall asleep." Col. Fitzwilliam eyes fell shut and he pillowed his head on his hands.

"Now, I certainly cannot decide, so I will name...Bishop Blarney to do so, in my stead."

Mr. Pierce marched to the top of the room. "Given the circumstances, I must insist you all come to church for I may never have such an audience to command again. Now you," he pointed to Mr. Darcy and Col. Fitzwilliam, "must make ready the chapel whilst I greet the people."

Mr. Pierce stooped over like an old man, glasses balanced on the edge of his nose, and shook hands with every person in the room. Mr. Darcy and Col. Fitzwilliam led the men in arranging the furniture into a fair semblance of a chapel.

Mr. Pierce shuffled to the bookstand-cum-pulpit and cleared his throat. "Hmmm, with so many fine folk here, it seems a shame to conduct an ordinary service—"

"I know! Let us have a wedding!" Louisa cried.

"Oh, let us do." Jane clapped softly.

"We may do so only if someone can produce a special license as I have not read the banns." Mr. Pierce wagged his finger at the crowd.

"For that you may trust your liege." Bingley pulled a paper from his coat and gave it to Mr. Pierce with a flourish. "You will find all is in order for your King to marry his Queen." He extended his hand to Kitty. She took it and he drew her closer.

Mr. Pierce squinted at the paper, taking far longer than he should for the sake of the skit. Creases lined his forehead, and his lips moved as he read. "You are correct. All is in order. Miss Bennet…" He lifted his gaze to her and nodded toward the paper, extending it slightly toward her.

Bingley's expression lost its puppy playfulness. He raised his brows and cocked his head.

She sucked in a sharp breath and leaned in. "It is real?" Her whisper barely escaped.

"It is." Mr. Pierce would not make a joke of something so sacred.

"Will you marry me, here and now, Kitty Bennet, with all of your friends, neighbors and family to share our joy?" Bingley squeezed her hand.

"I...I...it is so..."

"I know. Everyone shall remember and talk of it. No one will ever forget your wedding."

Nor would anyone think of Lydia anymore! Thoughtful, dear, wonderful man! Who else could conceive, much less orchestrate, such an extravagant gift?

"Yes, absolutely yes, I will marry you here and now." She dabbed her eyes with her handkerchief.

Bingley whooped and grabbed her waist. He whirled her about, her skirt trailing out behind her. A cheer rose from his brothers-to-be. Whispers rippled through the crowd.

"A little order and decorum, please. Let us recall this is a holy ordinance." Pierce rapped on the bookstand.

Mary looped her arm in Kitty's "Who shall stand up with you?"

"Louisa, please." Kitty glanced over her shoulder into Louisa's broad smile.

"Nothing would please me more."

Mary led Kitty to the back of the room where Papa waited, eyes twinkling.

"You knew?"

"He told me of his intentions and presented me with settlement papers. He may be impulsive, but he is thorough."

"And you approve?"

"What is wrong with providing our neighbors years of conversation whilst seeing you wed to a fine young man." He tucked her hand into the crook of his elbow. "I believe you shall be very happy."

Bingley took his place at the front of the church, Mr. Darcy standing with him. Mr. Pierce signaled and Papa slowly walked her down the make-shift aisle.

They all stared at her. Their friends and neighbors rejoiced for her, with her. Some were even a little envious. Her wedding had all the romance of an elopement, but none of the stain. She was marrying a man who loved her and she loved in return. What more could she want?

Mr. Pierce peered over his glasses. "Wilt thou have this Man to be thy wedded Husband, to live together after God's ordinance in the holy estate of Matrimony? Wilt thou obey him, and serve him, love, honor, and keep him in sickness and in health; and, forsaking all others, keep thee only unto him, so long as ye both shall live?"

Kitty swallowed hard and whispered, "I will." Tears trickled down her cheeks. Bingley caught them on his thumb. The next few moments blurred together.

He slipped a ring on her finger. "With this Ring I thee wed, with my Body I thee worship, and with all my worldly Goods I thee endow: In the Name of the Father, and of the Son, and of the Holy Ghost. Amen."

Mr. Pierce took their hands in his. "Let us pray. Eternal God, Creator and Preserver of all mankind, send thy blessing upon these thy servants, this Man and this Woman, whom we bless in thy Name; and may they ever remain in perfect love and peace together, and live according to thy laws, through Jesus

Christ our Lord. Those whom God hath joined together, let no man put asunder.

"Forasmuch as they have consented together in holy Wedlock, and have witnessed the same before God and this company, and thereto have given and pledged their troth either to the other, and have declared the same by giving and receiving of a Ring, and by joining of hands; I pronounce that they be Man and Wife together, In the Name of the Father, and of the Son, and of the Holy Ghost. Amen."

Bingley edged close and kissed her far longer than strictly proper, but this was Twelfth Night, an evening for wondrous things to occur.

Acknowledgments

So many people have helped me along the journey taking this from an idea to a reality. Abigail, Cassandra, Jan, Susan and Gerri thank you so much for cold reading and being honest!, Jan your proofreading is worth your weight in gold! And my dear friend Cathy my biggest cheerleader, you have kept me from chickening out more than once! Thank you!

Don't miss the rest of the

Given Good Principles Series
by Maria Grace

Darcy's Decision
The Future Mrs. Darcy
All the Appearance of Goodness

Available in paperback, e-book, and audiobook format at
all online bookstores.

Don't miss the free e-book
Bits of Bobbin Lace

with bonus chapters from the series

Download free at

RandomBitsofFascination.com

Though Maria Grace has been writing fiction since she was ten years old, those early efforts happily reside in a file drawer and are unlikely to see the light of day again, for which many are grateful.

She has one husband, two graduate degrees and two black belts, three sons, four undergraduate majors, five nieces, six pets, seven Regency-era fiction projects and notes for eight more writing projects in progress. To round out the list, she cooks for nine in order to accommodate the growing boys and usually makes ten meals at a time so she only cooks twice a month.

She can be contacted at:
email: author.MariaGrace@gmail.com.
Facebook: facebook.com/AuthorMariaGrace
On Amazon.com: amazon.com/author/mariagrace
Random Bits of Fascination
 (RandomBitsofFascination.com)
On Twitter @WriteMariaGrace
English Historical Fiction Authors
 (EnglshHistoryAuthors.blogspot.com)
Austen Authors (AustenAuthors.net)

29285828R00113

Made in the USA
Lexington, KY
21 January 2014